Trapped

in Grand

Falls

Cheryl Wright

Copyright

Trapped in Grand Falls
(Book One, Christmas Bride Dilemma)
This is book one of a multi-author series

Copyright ©2023 by Cheryl Wright

Cover Artist: Nancy Fraser

Editing: Sarah Lamb Editing

Dedication

To Margaret Tanner, my very dear friend and fellow author, for her enduring encouragement and friendship.

To Alan, my husband of over forty-eight years, who has been a relentless supporter of my writing and dreams for many years.

To You, my wonderful readers, who encourage me to continue writing these stories. It is such a joy knowing so many of you enjoy reading my stories as much as I love writing them for you.

Table of Contents

Chapter One

Devil's Edge, Montana, 1880s

Abigail Brooks listened carefully.

The house was finally quiet. She'd heard the front door shut maybe an hour ago, perhaps longer, after she'd heard the clip-clop of horses hooves heading into the barn. It wasn't long until she heard the bedroom door close, and there had been no sound since. Did that mean it was safe to make her move?

She pulled on her coat and gloves, then carefully slid open the window.

She winced at the creaking sound it made at first, but breathed a sigh of relief when it stopped a short time later. The icy wind blowing into the room had her shivering, despite her warm clothes and thick coat. Abigail pulled the collar up around her neck, then climbed out the window and into the snow.

Thankfully, it had only begun snowing in the past two days. It was not heavy, more flurries than anything. That meant she wouldn't leave evidence of which route she'd taken. It was an immense relief.

If only Abigail knew before what she knew now. Samuel Bosworth appeared to be a kind man, a caring man. He'd taken her to supper and brought her gifts. Nothing overly expensive, but nice things she would never have brought for herself. He treated her with respect, and Abigail was falling in love with him.

When he asked her to marry him, Abigail was thrilled. She'd never felt this way before, and never had a man paid her this kind of attention.

Then he took her home to meet his parents.

Her first clue about trouble was almost the moment they arrived. The cottage appeared empty. There was no light showing through the windows, despite the lateness of the day. No smoke coming from the chimney, and no one greeted them at the door.

A shiver ran through her as he lovingly helped her down from the buggy, then guided her to the front door. Samuel pulled out a key and unlocked it.

That was the moment Abigail realized something was very wrong.

As he turned the key in the door, she glanced about. Abigail looked for an escape, but there was none. They were in the middle of nowhere—well outside the town's edge. No matter where she looked, there was absolutely nowhere to run.

He picked her up and carried Abigail gently over the threshold. Had he believed crossing the front door with her meant they were man and wife? Something inside her shifted at that moment, and Abigail was at first fearful, then suddenly terrified. Her entire body trembled.

What did he have planned for her?

Samuel lit a lantern, indicated for her to sit down, then lit the fire. He then left the cottage, locking the door behind him. Scared witless, Abigail ran to the window watching his every move.

The gentle man, who had moments ago kidnapped her, patted his horse, then led it toward the barn. It was as though there were two sides to him.

What he would do next, Abigail did not know. She knew, however, she must escape.

Abigail's senses were on high alert. Every moment she delayed her escape meant possible recapture. Samuel towered over her and could easily control her.

Not that he'd harmed her as she'd predicted. He'd turned her into a slave. She cooked and cleaned for him. That first night, she was afraid he would force himself on her, but thankfully he didn't.

In Samuel's mind, they were all but married. He'd even produced a wedding ring for her to wear.

At first, she thought it was a joke. Until he showed Abigail her room, then left her alone. When the house was quiet and she believed him to be asleep, she ran to the front door. He'd padlocked it, and she couldn't get out. She recalled how far from town it was—how would she get back if she did escape? It was too far to walk, and Samuel would likely find her somewhere along the way. The only option was to go along with him for now and work out a solid plan.

Abigail pulled her coat up around herself. She knew it would be cold, but what choice did she have? When she arrived, the windows were unmovable. She had tried relentlessly, but they wouldn't budge. Whether they'd been jammed closed on purpose or it was accidental, she didn't know. What Abigail knew was she had to find a way to force her bedroom window open.

Sneaking a knife into her skirt pocket hadn't been easy, and at one point she was certain Samuel had noticed. She slowly and quietly chipped away at her bedroom window night after night until finally it gave way.

Moving quietly through the night, she now crept into the barn. Samuel's bedroom was on the far side of the house, away from the barn, which should mean a clean escape. She prayed it did.

Bluebell stared at her and whinnied as Abigail approached, then leaned in for a pat. Moving as quickly as she could, Abigail saddled the horse, then walked her out of the barn.

She was acutely aware Samuel may wake from the sounds of her riding out in the night's silence. They were on the edge of the forest before she mounted the horse. Snatching up a lantern as she left had been a good move. It was pitch black, and the forest was dense. Without it, Abigail could be in dire straits. Going from one desperate situation to another was not part of her plan.

As if by instinct, Bluebell rode toward town. Abigail would go straight to the sheriff's office, but with Samuel being such an *upstanding citizen*, would the sheriff even believe her? She'd been gone several days at least, so may not have even been reported as missing.

Abigail's heart sank. Perhaps she would be better off quietly leaving town and making a life elsewhere?

The closer to town they got, the lighter it became. Watching the sunrise was an amazing sight, and Abigail reveled in the display before her. It wouldn't be long and she would arrive at Devil's Edge, her home of the past three years.

By the time Bluebell stopped outside the sheriff's office, Abigail was exhausted. She simply wanted to sleep, but couldn't. Once Samuel realized she was missing, he would come looking for her. She couldn't linger and ran inside, where the sheriff was asleep in his chair. She stood there for a long moment watching him sleep. He continued to snore and fury built up inside her.

"Sheriff!" Abigail knew she'd shouted, but she couldn't help it. Time was of the essence.

He shook himself awake. "Wha…?" The sheriff opened his eyes and glanced about. Too bad if it was a life and death situation, and to Abigail, it was.

She sat down opposite the indifferent sheriff and told him the entire miserable story. It was obvious she was not believed.

"The Bosworths are good people. The stagecoach will be here in…" he pulled out his pocket watch. "Thirty minutes. I suggest you get yourself a ticket. There's enough time for you to grab some belongings and meet the stage—provided you hurry." He stood then and made himself a coffee.

Abigail's fury turned to fiery anger. How did this man call himself a lawman? She had little choice but to do as he suggested. She ran to her small apartment above the mercantile, grabbed what she could in the short time available, and snatched up the wad of money she had hidden away where no one could find it.

As she shoved the notes into her reticule, Abigail knew they would be her saving grace.

On the road to nowhere, Abigail kept to herself. Telling other passengers her woeful story was not something she intended to do.

She glanced about at the few people who shared the carriage. Two elderly women who introduced themselves as sisters were far older than Abigail. A middle-aged cowboy on his way to a ranch he'd worked at before, and a preacher going to a new placement.

At least it was warm inside. Her trip into town had been harrowing to say the least. Before she'd even arrived, Abigail somehow knew what sort of reception she would get from the sheriff. The man was lazy and rarely did anything to keep the peace. The town had certainly lived up to its name. She should have steered clear of Devil's Edge. She'd never intended to stay there, but liked what she saw.

The name should have sent out a warning, but she didn't heed it.

"Where are you headed, dear?" one sister asked quietly. The two women had chatted between themselves for the past two hours, and Abigail had hoped they would stop for breath. What she hadn't counted on was the fact they might turn to her instead.

Abigail glanced out the window as she tried to think of a plausible answer. She hadn't noticed how heavy the snow had become. It was, after all, December, so should have been no surprise. She'd read for most of the journey, which was well into its third day. "I, um…" She didn't want to disclose anything, but how could she refuse? "I'm on my way to visit a cousin," she said, realizing she was floundering but not sure how to address the issue. Abigail truly did not know where she was headed. Nor would she want to share the information if she did.

"Oh, that will be lovely for you both," the woman said.

Out of the blue, they were all thrown sideways. Abigail was trapped underneath one of the well-proportioned sisters, and the preacher was thrown to the floor. No one was spared, with the cowboy flanked by the other sister, and the preacher piled on the other two. The stagecoach was barely upright and was rocking precariously, but was surprisingly still standing.

Desperate to reunite, the elderly sisters clasped each other's hands, then huddled together the moment they were reunited. The cowboy, seemingly far more calm than anyone else, made his way back to his seat, then opened the carriage door and glanced about. The preacher prayed for them all. Abigail felt truly alone at that moment, but did and said nothing. Out of pure luck, or perhaps lack of space, she was still in one piece. As far as she could tell, no one was seriously injured.

Her heart thudded, and her entire body shook. Were they attacked? She did not know what had occurred, and she was certain no one else did either.

"Everything seems in order," the cowboy announced as he closed the door. "At least it's not a robbery. We might have hit a rock?" He sat back in his seat and waited with the rest of the passengers, who were now upright and resettled where they were before their worlds tilted.

Abigail couldn't help but stare at the snow that fell relentlessly. How far were they from a town? Not too far, she hoped, but wasn't convinced that would be the case. Her biggest fear was being stuck out in the middle of nowhere. She did not know if stagecoach robberies took place out here in the wilderness, but prayed they would all be safe.

Surely if that were the case, she would have heard about it from the other passengers?

The stagecoach rocked again, slowly at first, then it groaned and moved sideways. The passengers collectively gasped. The preacher continued to pray. Abigail heard the driver grunting as he moved around the stagecoach until finally he opened the door and clumsily climbed inside. "Is anyone hurt?" he asked, glancing about the interior.

"Everyone seems fine," the old cowboy said, as his eyes roamed from passenger to passenger.

"The wheel is broken," their driver, Benjamin Diamond announced, his irritation clear. "We have no choice but to disembark. I'm afraid we'll have to walk to the next town." He pulled his collar up against the icy wind and snow, then climbed outside again.

The others all glanced from one passenger to the other. What they thought about it made no difference—it wouldn't change the outcome. The cowboy was the first to move. "Put on your coats and gloves, everyone," he commanded. "It's cold out there."

Abigail almost laughed. It was snowing, of course it was cold. She refrained, not wanting to give anyone a poor impression. Instead, she stood and pulled on her coat and gloves as best she could in the confined space. She wasn't convinced they would do much against this ghastly weather. They could only hope the next town wasn't far away.

The cowboy, Walt, he said his name was, climbed out first, and helped the ladies down the few steps. Benjamin, their driver, was unloading small bags and handing them to their owners. He then worked to remove the faulty wheel. Walt unhitched the horses and led them through the snow.

Abigail was distraught. The wheel would have to be repaired before they could continue their trip. She didn't know if the stagecoach itself was damaged. If that were the case, they might have a long stay-over before continuing on their way.

"The town isn't too much further," Benjamin told them as they trudged through the snow. "This snow makes it a slow trip, but I'm afraid we have no choice. At least it isn't knee deep."

"Couldn't you leave us here to wait?" the older of the two sisters asked.

Even Abigail knew that wasn't possible. With the wheel no longer attached, the stagecoach tipped at a dangerous angle.

"Afraid not, Miss." The answer came swiftly, and she empathized with the woman's disappointment. "It isn't far, up around the bend," Benjamin said, pointing ahead.

"The townsfolk are very friendly. You can get a decent meal there, but accommodation could be a problem," cowboy Walt said. He had obviously visited there before.

"Excuse me," Abigail whispered. "What is the name of this town?"

"It's called Grand Falls, Miss. You're sure to like it."

Chapter Two

The driver was right—Grand Falls seemed like a nice place.

They'd headed straight for the diner where they could warm up. There was a roaring fire, and everyone huddled around it. The diner owner seemed nice, and the food was delicious. The best Abigail had experienced since her journey out of Devil's Edge.

As they'd been warned, Grand Falls had little in the way of accommodation. There was a men's boarding house, and they could accommodate the male passengers and workers, but not the women.

The three women were told not to worry, and they would be placed with locals. Abigail was astonished. She'd never been to a town where the townsfolk were willing to help out in such a way. Being seated so close to the fire suited Abigail, as it had the others caught in the same predicament. How long they would have to stay, she didn't know.

Living under the roof and off the generosity of strangers didn't sit well with her.

Especially after her recent ordeal.

Abigail brought her napkin to her lips. The food far exceeded anything she'd ever tasted before. The diner was warm and welcoming, and the owner bent over backwards to help. "Accommodation is being arranged for you three ladies as we speak," Tucker Smith, the diner's owner, told them. "I'll let you know the moment there's any news." He filled their mugs with coffee, then left the group alone.

"I hope we can stay together," Abigail told the sisters.

It was clear the two did not want to be separated. "I go wherever my sister goes," Gertrude, the younger of the sisters, said firmly. Abigail completely understood that. She was privately afraid of being whisked away on her own. Surely they wouldn't place her somewhere by herself? She shivered despite the warmth of the fire.

The older sister, Maisy, wrapped Gertrude in a big hug. "Don't worry, sister. I'll make sure we're not forced apart." The two women held each other tightly. "Perhaps we can convince them to let you come with us too, Abigail?" Maisy said once the two women ended their embrace.

Abigail knew it was wishful thinking. "I hope so, but most likely not," she said sadly. "It is very kind of the townsfolk to offer to put us up, but I doubt their hospitality would stretch so far to take in three of us." She knew it was true, as much as she would prefer to be with these women she only met days ago. She felt safe with them. After her ordeal with Samuel Bosworth, Abigail was more than a little wary of strangers.

Her quiet reflection was interrupted by their host, who carried a tray loaded with assorted muffins. "Help yourselves," he said, placing the tray in the center of the table.

"Thank you," Abigail said quietly. She might be afraid, and unsure of her future, but her manners were still intact. "Do you have any idea where I might end up?" She felt heat rise in her cheeks as everyone turned to stare at her. Was she being pushy? Or even selfish? Abigail didn't think so. Maisy and Gertrude had each other. She had no one. That meant she had to look out for herself.

Tucker turned to face her. "I understand your concern," he said respectfully. Abigail was afraid he might be angry, even a little. Thankfully, he wasn't. "Please don't worry yourself. I've sent a message to someone I'm almost certain can help." He smiled at her then, and Abigail knew he was trying to reassure her.

Moments later, the entrance to the diner flew open. Snow blew inside, and with it came Benjamin Diamond—their stagecoach driver. The man looked chilled to the bone.

Tucker lifted a hand and waved him over to their table, handing him a steaming mug of coffee. "Sit yourself down," he said. "Or warm up at the fire. Either way, I'll get you something hot to eat."

"Thank you, Tucker," their driver said. "I appreciate it. Well," he said, addressing everyone around the table, "the wheel is at the blacksmith's shop. It's pretty mangled, so we could be stuck here for some time."

The sisters gasped and clasped their hands together. "What about the rest of our belongings?" Gertrude asked, her voice shaking.

"Depending on the weather, I'll get a few men together tomorrow, and we'll ride out and collect everything left behind. I don't expect stage robbers will be out in this weather. Besides, they are not interested in ladies' intimate wear," he said with a smile. "They want gold and cash, and there is none."

He turned back to the fire and sipped his coffee. Until now, Abigail hadn't noticed how tall he was, nor how broad his shoulders were. In fact, she'd barely noticed their stagecoach driver at all. Likely because they had little interaction with him during their trip. The main time they saw him was at the various stops along the way. He kept to himself, just as Abigail had done most of the trip.

Even once the accident occurred, he didn't say much, but ensured everyone was safe and arrived in town without incident.

She shivered despite the warmth emanating from the fire. Benjamin stoked the logs, and the flames grew higher. She reveled in the additional warmth. It made her wonder why she didn't take the train. They had a train station here in Grand Falls. Or so she'd been told.

The answer was that Devil's Edge held no such luxury, and the stage was the only way out of her predicament. Little did she know they would all be unceremoniously hurled onto each other, and made to walk through the snow, ultimately to safety.

"Are you alright, dear?" Maisy's gentle voice cut through Abigail's thoughts. She turned to face the much older woman and found herself shaking her head. What a foolish girl she was. She was far too trusting, and look where that had got her.

Now she was running for her life. Abigail had no way of knowing whether Samuel would track her down. There was a time when she believed she knew him, thought him a good person. Samuel ensured that opinion changed the moment he kidnapped her. Despite what the sheriff said, she had been kidnapped.

"When a person is held against their will, locked away with no means of escape, that is kidnapping."

"What is that you said, dear? You were kidnapped?" Maisy's voice held incredulity, and Abigail's head shot up.

Had she really said the words out loud? Abigail swallowed. Hard. Should she tell the truth or try to wriggle her way out of this? "Kidnapped? Do I look like I've been kidnapped?" Abigail whispered. She laughed then, trying to hide the truth from her new friend.

Maisy smiled, but Abigail felt it was forced. "No, you really don't." She laughed, but again, Abigail wasn't certain the laughter was genuine. She didn't want anyone to know what had happened to her. If word got around Grand Falls, would word somehow get back to Samuel Bosworth she was trapped here?

A shiver went down Abigail's spine. The last thing she wanted, or needed, was to have her kidnapper learn where she was. The sooner the stagecoach was fixed, the better. When that happened, she could move on. Where that would be, and how long she'd be able to stay there, was another question altogether. What she really needed was anonymity. Finding a place to hide where no one knew her, or what she'd been through. That would be the safest way to hide from Samuel.

Perhaps Abigail could take on another identity? She shivered again. Would she ever be free to be herself again, or would she be forever on the run?

Her heart thudded, and she felt ill. The thought of spending the rest of her days trying to keep safe did not appease Abigail. She had always lived a quiet life. She'd mostly kept to herself, and been a stellar citizen, no matter where she lived.

One moment her life was going along fine, the next she was a prisoner. There was no rhyme nor reason to what occurred—Abigail simply couldn't fathom why Samuel had locked her away. There was only one explanation she could think of. It had to be the man was crazy.

Chapter Three

Benjamin glanced over at the passengers he'd let down. He knew the road like the back of his hand, and yet, he'd still broken a wheel.

He knew fully that rock was there, but with the road covered in snow, he'd been unable to avoid it. He admonished himself. There was no excuse for putting his passengers in danger. He didn't care about the wheel, that was an easy fix. It was pure luck no one was injured.

As he glanced about, his eyes stopped at Miss Brooks. There was something about her that caught his eye from the moment they met. If he didn't know better, he'd say she was hiding something. In his line of business, he'd learned to read people. It was clear something was amiss with the young woman, but what it was, he'd probably never know.

Tucker interrupted his thoughts when he brought a hot meal to the table. "Here you go, Ben," he said, then motioned for the passengers to come closer. "I have arranged accommodation for everyone."

There was a sigh of relief from the group. "Except for you, Miss Brooks. I'm still waiting to hear back." He went on to explain the arrangements, and everyone nodded their approval.

Ben was certain he knew who would accommodate the lone woman, but didn't comment—it wasn't his place.

"I'm sorry, dear," Maisy, the older sister, said quietly. "I'm certain you'll be well looked after."

He watched as the younger woman's face paled. No matter what scenario ran through his mind, Ben was certain there was something amiss. Every passenger had been displaced, but she was the only one who seemed to be distraught over the situation. What was he missing?

The door to the diner opened, and snow blew inside. Edna Baker quickly entered, accompanied by Joseph Davis, town bootmaker, and Mrs. Baker's friend.

She hurried over to their table, her eyes studying each passenger. She murmured something to Tucker, then moved toward Miss Abigail Brooks. It was no surprise to Ben to discover Mrs. Baker had been asked to accommodate the single woman.

"Miss Brooks?" the older woman said when she was standing beside her intended target. "I'm Edna Baker. You will be staying with me for the duration." She studied the young woman, who said not a word, but Ben heard her sigh of relief. "You'll be safe with me," Mrs. Baker said gently.

A barely visible smile crossed Abigail's lips. "Thank you, Mrs. Baker. I appreciate your generous offer."

Despite her words, Ben heard the reluctance in her voice. Apparently Mrs. Baker did too, since she frowned. Edna Baker was well-known for taking in strays, and tonight was no different. The former diner owner had sheltered several young women over the years. Many had eventually settled in Grand Falls. Some had even married here and had a family.

It was certainly a wonderful place to raise children. Not that he had personal experience in that regard. As a stagecoach driver, he was often away from home. It was not conducive to settling down. Although he did call Grand Falls home for the short time he was here.

"My offer still stands," he told Tucker. "I can accommodate the two men if needed."

Tucker put a hand to his back. "There is room at the boarding house. Besides, you have enough to worry about. Apart from a broken wheel, you'll have to retrieve your stagecoach. That won't be a simple task."

Ben nodded. What he said was true. It wasn't something Ben was looking forward to, but would have to be done sooner rather than later. The snow would only get heavier. "Depending on the weather, I'll make a trip out there tomorrow and retrieve everyone's luggage. If I can get a few men together, I can hopefully get the stagecoach upright again."

Tucker didn't hesitate with an offer. "I'll come with you. I'm certain my brother Charlie will be happy to come along, too."

"Count me in," Joseph said. "The more hands, the better, right?"

Warmth flooded Ben. He loved this town. It might be expanding with all the newcomers that seemed to flock here, but it was still the best place in the world to live. "Thank you, both. I appreciate your offers. How does nine o'clock sound?" Both men agreed, and Ben went back to his food.

Abigail studied him. Perhaps she didn't realize he owned the stage line? It certainly wasn't something he made a big song and dance about with his passengers. He simply did his job—sold the tickets, greeted the passengers and stored their luggage, then drove them to their destination. That was the extent of his contact with his passengers. Until today.

Breaking a wheel had not only displaced and dismayed his passengers, but it was bound to cost him a lot of lost time. Not to mention money. Still, he knew it was always a risk when he started his own stage line. So far, his business was small, but expansion was on the horizon. He had two other drivers and stagecoaches, and business was going well. He cared for his horses well, and also his staff. Without them, he wouldn't have a business.

Mrs. Baker sat down next to him. "How are you holding up, Mr. Diamond?" she asked, her concern clear.

Ben put down his cutlery. "I'll be fine. I'm more concerned about my passengers," he told her truthfully.

"Of course you are, dear, but our Tucker has it all in hand." She smiled at him then. Tucker was always good in a disaster. He had a knack for pulling everything together and managing all the details.

"He does, and for that, I am truly grateful." Ben hoped and prayed Tucker understood how thankful he was for the man's expertise in making arrangements for everyone. It was a huge load off *his* shoulders.

"Miss Brooks, if you are ready, we will go. Mr. Davis will accompany us back to my little cottage to ensure we get there safely."

"Thank you both," Abigail said. "I can't thank you enough."

She still appeared concerned, but it was understandable. Not only had Abigail been unceremoniously dumped from her seat in a stagecoach which had lurched sideways, she'd been forced to trudge through the freezing snow, not knowing where she would end up. To give her due, she had not once complained. Almost the entire trip, the two sisters grumbled about the cold and their skirts getting wet.

Still, there was little he'd been able to do about it. Accidents happen, and the results were unpredictable. Ben was more than a little grateful they weren't attacked by robbers, which was a hazard of the job. He prayed when they drove out to the stagecoach tomorrow the baggage was still there. Grand Falls was quite isolated, so they might be in luck. If they weren't, there was nothing he could do to change the fact.

Mrs. Baker stood, bringing Ben back to the present. "Goodnight, everyone. Take care," she said, her gaze taking in everyone at his table. "We will surely see each other again tomorrow."

Abigail stood. She seemed relieved. Perhaps because she now knew where she would stay and with whom? Mrs. Baker was harmless, but Abigail didn't know that. At least she didn't know it before. Surely she understood it now?

"Goodnight, everyone," Abigail said as she pulled on her coat and gloves. The two sisters hurried over and hugged her. It was strange the friendships that were struck up after a few days in a stagecoach together.

Joseph Davis hurried to the diner door, ready to open it. Sensibly, he waited until the ladies arrived to avoid another influx of snow assaulting the room. He pulled up the collar of his coat moments before he opened the door, and the trio hurried out.

Chapter Four

The snow hit Abigail in the face as they left the diner. Instead of being lighter, the snow seemed far heavier than it was when they trudged into town. She should be grateful for the reprieve they had earlier. If the snow had been this heavy at the time, would the horses have made it? She wasn't convinced. It had been quite difficult for them as it was.

Mrs. Baker reached out and hooked her arm through Abigail's. "How are you coping, dear?" She was shouting, although Abigail had no idea why. She glanced across at Mr. Davis, who was grinning.

"I am better now I know where I am going." She sighed with relief again, but Abigail wouldn't feel truly relieved until she was in Mrs. Baker's cottage and saw her surroundings for herself.

"Of course you are, dear. I can understand that." Mrs. Baker patted her gloved hand, and Abigail appreciated the other woman's words.

Glancing up, Abigail saw a cottage not far ahead, and wondered if it was Mrs. Baker's home. "Nearly there," Mrs. Baker said, patting her hand again.

Abigail hoped and prayed there was a roaring fire waiting for them inside. She was chilled to the bone, despite the coat and gloves she wore. She had been able to dry out her skirts by the fire at the diner, but now they were wet again. Thankfully, she had a small bag with a few changes of clothes.

She gasped. "I forgot my luggage," she declared, unable to hide her dismay. Mr. Davis lifted his arm, displaying her carpetbag. Relief flooded Abigail—her bag was not forgotten—at least by this wonderful man. Tears danced on her lashes, and her chin quivered. It was all too much. Abigail wanted to get inside and hide away from these two generous people who had risked their own safety to ensure she was safe and warm.

Mrs. Baker unlocked the door, then put a hand to Abigail's back, guiding her inside. "It's alright, Miss Brooks. You are safe here. I'll look after you." She glanced across at Mr. Davis. "This town will look after you and the other passengers. This was the perfect place for the accident to happen."

Warmth hit Abigail in the face. She stepped into the small sitting room, which was directly inside the door. There was an enormous fireplace, and several large logs burned fiercely. Abigail was drawn to the fire, and hurried toward it.

Mr. Davis came inside and placed her bag near the door. "I'll leave you ladies now," he said, rubbing his gloved hands together. "The missus will be waiting." Moments later, before Abigail could thank him, he was gone.

Abigail pulled off her coat and gloves and swiped at her eyes. As silly as it was, tears flooded her cheeks. She was safe. She was here in this warm cottage with a caring woman who promised to look after her until she could leave on the stagecoach again.

Abigail felt an arm go up around her. The petite woman, who was decades older than her, was endeavoring to comfort her. "It's a lot to take in, I know," she said gently. "You've been through a lot."

More than you'll ever know, Abigail wanted to say, but refrained. It sounded ridiculous to her own mind. She couldn't imagine what a complete stranger would think about recent events in Devil's Edge. Even the sheriff there didn't believe her. Of course, the man was a fool.

Swiping at her tears again, Abigail nodded. She didn't trust herself to speak.

"Let me show you to your room. You can get settled, then if you want to, come back to the fire. Or stay here for now."

"Thank you," Abigail whispered. Her tears had stopped, but she knew they could start again at any moment. Her mind was in a whirl, and her heart was hollow.

Mrs. Baker turned and led Abigail to her temporary room. It was small, but homely and welcoming. "It's lovely, thank you," Abigail said, her eyes taking in all aspects of the room she would call home for a day or two. "I do appreciate your offer," Abigail said, then reached into her reticule. Her hand outstretched, she offered the woman a handful of banknotes. "Is this enough to cover your costs?" she asked. "I have more if needed."

Her hostess frowned. "Put that away," she said gruffly. "I don't want your money. I am doing this out of the goodness of my heart, as any Christian would."

Abigail felt bad. She'd offended her hostess. "I apologize," she said quietly. "Honestly, I didn't mean anything by it. I simply don't want you to be out of pocket."

Waving a hand in front of her, Mrs. Baker grimaced, then looked her up and down. "You are a slip of a girl. I doubt you'll eat my life savings." She laughed then. "I used to own the diner," she said, then walked out of the room.

What a strange thing for the woman to say. Was Abigail supposed to take that as meaning the woman was rich? She glanced about. Her home didn't portray richness. It was more along the lines of what she would expect of a middle-class widow. She'd assumed Mrs. Baker was a widow, since another man back accompanied them to her cottage, and there was no Mr. Baker here.

Abigail sat on the side of the bed. It was soft and welcoming, and she couldn't wait to lie down and close her eyes. Right now, though, she needed to warm up more. Oh! And her bag was still in the sitting room.

When she pulled off her boots, her stockings were drenched, and the boots were soaked through. Abigail's feet were almost numb with the cold. She was certain Mrs. Baker would not mind her walking through the house barefooted under the circumstances. Would she? Removing the wet stockings, she picked up her boots and carried them out to the fire.

Mrs. Baker sat at the table, which wasn't far from the fire. "I made a hot cup of tea for you. Warm yourself up." She glanced down at the boots Abigail carried. "Put those next to the fire. They should dry overnight."

Abigail hoped so. They were the only boots she had. She'd left most of her belongings behind and would have to start over.

Morning came far too early for Abigail's liking.

She was used to getting up early, so it wasn't that. Yesterday had been exhausting and seemed to go on forever. The moment her head hit the pillow, she was sound asleep. But now, daylight slipped in between the curtains of the guest room at Mrs. Baker's cozy cottage. She could hear movement in the kitchen that wasn't far away, and guessed her hostess was busy preparing for the day.

There was a chill in the air, and she slid her feet into a pair of slippers loaned to her by Mrs. Baker. Her robe, although a little worse for the wear, was at the end of her bed. She glanced around the room as she got her bearings. At least she wasn't locked up in Samuel Bosworth's cottage, out in the middle of nowhere.

A shudder wracked her body, and Abigail kicked off the slippers and climbed back into bed. She then pulled the covers up to her chin. Facing each day had become a chore, but she knew today was a blessing. She was alive, and she was free from Samuel's clutches. How long it would last, she didn't know. That in itself was a problem.

A shadow came across her and a shiver went down her spine. It took a moment for Abigail to remember she was safe. Glancing across at the doorway, the small stature of Edna Baker stood there looking across at her. She was frowning.

"Is everything alright, Miss Brooks?" She stepped forward, then sat on the edge of the bed. She oozed compassion, and Abigail appreciated it. Still, Abigail wasn't sure she was ready to tell anyone what happened to her. The reaction from the sheriff was bad enough.

Forcing herself to smile, Abigail studied the older woman. "Everything is fine. I'm still half asleep, that's all. And it is so cold!"

Mrs. Baker glanced at her. There didn't seem to be much the woman missed. Still, she wasn't prepared to talk about her ordeal. Not now, not ever. The best thing Abigail could do for herself was keep moving. The worst thing that could happen was Samuel finding her. If he did, it could put the wonderful people of Grand Falls in danger. Abigail couldn't abide that. Each and every one had stepped up to help her and the other passengers. Not one had asked for anything in return. "Get up," she said, her eyes never leaving Abigail's, "when you're ready. The fire is hot and you can warm up there. I have oats on the stove. They're hot and creamy."

She stood then and left Abigail alone with her thoughts. There were times she felt Mrs. Baker could break into her mind and understand her every thought. Silly, really. No one could do that, but the woman seemed to know there was something amiss. Thankfully, Abigail would be gone from Grand Falls today. At least, she hoped she would be. Or tomorrow at the latest. It surely wouldn't take long for the stagecoach to be repaired.

Although she certainly wasn't an expert at such things.

She reluctantly pushed the covers back and once again slipped her feet into the slippers sitting beside her bed. She put on her robe again, almost ashamed to even be seen wearing it, then wandered out to the kitchen. Warmth filled the entire room, and she reveled in the coziness she felt there. Mrs. Baker stood at the woodstove, presumably stirring the oats.

"Ah, there you are," she said, smiling broadly, then poured the oats into two bowls, one for each woman. She poured tea into two mugs and put one in front of Abigail. The room was filled with delicious aromas. It was far too long since Abigail had sat in a kitchen like this. Even longer since anyone had fussed over her. She wasn't sure if that was a good thing, or if it was bad.

"Thank you," she said quietly, then waited for her hostess to sit at the table.

The moment she did, Mrs. Baker closed her eyes and gave thanks for their food. She also asked their Lord to bless Abigail in her future travels. Warmth flooded her, and she immediately felt safe.

"Tuck in while it's hot," Mrs. Baker said, then did just that.

The oats were both hot and very creamy, as promised. She sipped the tea. It was perfect—not too weak, and not too strong. "Thank you," Abigail said again. "The oats are perfect, the best I've ever had. You make a perfect cup of tea as well."

Mrs. Baker grinned. "I did own the diner for decades," she said. "Customers can be fussy. You learn to ensure everything is flawless after a while."

"Well, I appreciate it," Abigail said. "It's been a while since I've had a decent home-cooked meal." Except for her own cooking, that was. And she certainly wasn't the best cook. Samuel didn't complain, but what choice did he have? He'd held her prisoner, which meant she couldn't leave the cottage he'd turned into a makeshift prison.

The mere thought of it made Abigail gasp. As a result, she almost choked on her oats. Mrs. Baker studied her. "Are you alright, dear?" the older woman said, concern written all over her face.

"My… the food went down the wrong way," she whispered. "I'll be fine, thank you." Abigail wiped her lips with the linen napkin, her eyes never leaving her hostess' face. From the moment she'd met Edna Baker, Abigail knew she was going to have to be careful. She seemed like the sort of person who could entice confessions from complete strangers.

Abigail could not pin down her reason for that belief, but was certain it was true. Those piercing eyes seemed to confirm her assessment, but Mrs. Baker only nodded, then went back to eating. "Your gown is dry, but your boots are not quite ready," she said when her bowl was empty. "I do hope you have another pair with you."

"I'm afraid not," Abigail said.

Mrs. Baker studied her. "Mr. Diamond intends to collect the remaining luggage this morning, so you'll have your other belongings later today."

Abigail wasn't sure if she should respond. It was clear Mrs. Baker was not one to let things go. She took a deep and fortifying breath, then slowly let it out. "I have no other belongings," she finally said, knowing it would open a pandora's box.

Instead of answering, the older woman studied her, far more than before. A frown creased her forehead, and she now appeared concerned. Mrs. Baker slid her hand across the table, then covered Abigail's hand. "What are you running from, dear?" She was blunt, Abigail would give her that.

Still, blunt or not, she didn't want to share her story. Knowing she'd already been disbelieved wasn't helping. Besides, how would Samuel find her here? Previously, she'd thought it a possibility, but now she wondered if she was overreacting. It was difficult to track a person down. Especially when you didn't know where they were heading.

She smiled tentatively, but Mrs. Baker continued to study her. The woman's dark eyes radiated into her soul. "Nothing," Abigail said, then bit her bottom lip. She was normally not one to bend the truth even a little. She hated telling this dear lady even a little white lie, let alone an outright one that might send her to hell.

"I understand," the small woman said quietly. "You don't know me. I could be a further danger for all you know." She slid her hand across the table again and patted Abigail's hand. She found it eerily comforting. Abigail's eyes opened wide in fear, and she pulled her hand away. Her heart pounding, Abigail stood, ready to run. She glanced about, getting her bearings.

She felt the other woman's eyes burn into her. "Everything is alright, Abigail. You are safe here, I promise."

With her heart still pounding, Abigail stood frozen to the spot. What were her options? Stay and take her chances, or run and end up goodness knew where. The latter was out—she couldn't leave Grand Falls under her own steam. The stagecoach was in a state of disrepair, and the train didn't leave until Monday. She was stuck here.

Pounding on the door startled her. Abigail was lightheaded and had to sit down again. Mrs. Baker stood. "I'll see who that is," she whispered, placing a gentle hand on Abigail's shoulder. "Why don't you get dressed, then come into the sitting room?"

Bracing herself to stand again, Abigail nodded. If she was in danger, the last thing she needed was to be caught in her nightclothes. Not that she knew where to run if that was her only option. Her wayward thoughts brought Abigail to the conclusion she needed to roam the town. Look around and work out the layout of the place. If she needed to hide, where would she go? Did they have a sheriff here, and if so, was he any better than the one at Devil's Edge?

Her mind was in turmoil. Her life was in danger. Abigail needed a plan to save her life.

Chapter Five

Ben pounded on Mrs. Baker's door. He needed to check how many pieces of luggage Abigail Brooks had, to ensure nothing was left behind.

When the door finally opened, Mrs. Baker appeared frazzled. It wasn't something he was used to seeing. She was normally calm and happy. Right now, she seemed quite concerned. "Good morning, Mr. Diamond." She opened the door wider and ushered him inside. "Come in out of the cold."

Ben strode straight for the fire and pulled off his heavy coat and gloves. "Thank you, Mrs. Baker," he said. "Good morning to you, too." He shuddered then. He was chilled to the bone. This weather was not conducive to the work ahead of him. The last thing he wanted was to drive out to his broken stagecoach and retrieve luggage. He knew, however, if he left it much longer, the luggage would be pilfered and his passengers would be furious.

"I gather you're looking for Miss Brooks," she said. "She won't be long. I'll get you a coffee while you wait." Mrs. Baker was gone before he had a chance to respond. As much as he needed to be on his way, the offer of coffee was certainly appreciated. He rubbed his frozen hands near the fire, endeavoring to warm them up.

He heard barely audible footsteps behind him. He turned to find Abigail Brooks standing there, a look of shock on her face. "Good morning," he said, trying to lessen her fright. She was a vision of beauty. Even at this hour of the day, when she was likely still half asleep. Or perhaps it was simply the fact he had turned up when she had least expected a visitor.

As his eyes roamed from her head down to her toes, he noticed her feet were bare. He stepped forward to greet her and tripped. Steadying himself, Ben glanced down. There stood a pair of dainty boots. He had no idea why, but a smile came to his lips. "Yours?" he asked, still grinning.

She frowned. "They're wet." Despite her words, Abigail leaned down and picked them up, pushing her hand inside one boot. She sighed then, so presumably they were still wet.

"I'll be collecting the rest of your luggage soon," he said, glancing at the boots to stop himself from staring at the beauty standing before him. "How many pieces…"

"There is none," she said bluntly. "I was traveling light." Heat moved up her face and reddened her cheeks. Ben felt guilty for asking. He'd obviously embarrassed her, and it was the last thing he'd intended.

At that moment, Mrs. Baker returned, carrying a mug of steaming coffee, and handed it to him. "Thank you," he said, then sat down as indicated by his hostess.

"You will be careful out there today, won't you?" Mrs. Baker was worried for his safety, that much was clear.

"We will. I won't be alone. Tucker and a few of the other men have offered to help." He took a long sip of the hot beverage he held in his hands. It was good. Everyone knew Mrs. Baker made the best coffee when she owned the diner, but he didn't realize she still did so at home. "This is excellent coffee," he said, glancing her way.

She threw him a sly smile. "Of course it is." She turned away then and left him alone with Abigail.

"How are you feeling today?" he asked. She seemed out of sorts last night. Most likely because of the situation she found herself in. The sisters were able to stay together, but Abigail was plucked out of the group to go home alone with a stranger.

She turned from where she was warming her hands at the fire and studied him. Then she licked her lips as though she needed time to think through her answer. Her solemn expression suddenly turned to a smile. One that didn't reach her eyes and clearly wasn't genuine. "I'm fine," she said, her voice barely above a whisper. "Mrs. Baker is lovely." Ben noticed her hands were shaking. It couldn't be from the cold—she surely hadn't been outside. Her feet were bare, and her boots drying next to the burning logs.

Abigail Brooks was a curiosity. Probably one he would never understand. Certainly not in the short time he would get to spend with her. "I'm sorry your trip was cut short," he said, feeling bad for stranding her in Grand Falls. Not that it was a terrible place to be stuck—it was probably the best place they could have been trapped in. It suited him, that was for sure. He could climb into his own bed last night, and had slept better than he had for a while.

Ben had grown up here and felt privileged to do so. The townsfolk had always been kind and supportive, and many had given him advice on running a business. Mrs. Baker was one of them. As she was a successful diner owner, he had listened carefully. She was a shrewd businesswoman, and no one could deny that.

He glanced at Abigail again. Her face was pale. More than pale, she was ghostly white. He wondered why that could be. A day or two from her schedule surely wouldn't cause her grief? Or perhaps it would. She could be on her way to start a job as a governess or a schoolteacher for all he knew. "I can send a telegraph to whomever you need. Let them know you'll arrive late." She gazed at him but didn't say a word. "At my cost, of course. This is my fault, and I'll bear the price."

Instead of relieved, she suddenly looked scared. No, she was terrified. What could Miss Abigail Brooks be hiding? Because it was crystal clear she was hiding something. The woman was petrified, and he wanted to know who had caused her to be that way. He stared at her over his mug and drank down the last of his coffee. Ben knew he had no choice but to leave. The others would be waiting for him at the livery. Then they would travel out to the stagecoach to retrieve everyone's luggage. Except for Abigail's—she had none.

The more he thought about it, the stranger it all seemed. Exactly who was Abigail Brooks, and what was she running from? The question was begging to be answered.

Tucker, his brother Charlie, and Joseph were all waiting for him when Ben arrived at the livery. Blacksmith Harrison Price was there too, which was a pleasant surprise. And not unwelcomed. He would have a far better idea about repairs needed than Ben would.

Charlie had the wagon hitched up with two horses. The other men would ride under their own steam. Each one wore a heavy coat and gloves, and a thick scarf around his neck. It was a miserable day, but while they could get through the snow, they would.

There was no way to predict how long it would be before they could be on their journey again if they didn't go today. If the weather worsened, and it surely would, it could be a week or more. With Christmas coming up, it wasn't surprising, but the snow was unusually thick.

Ben looked at the sky. They needed to get in and out as quickly as possible—everyone's safety was at risk if a storm suddenly hit. He climbed up onto the wagon and took the reins. "Let's go," he shouted, to ensure everyone heard, then flicked the reins.

It wasn't far to where the accident occurred, despite what it felt like when they'd had to walk through the snow the day before. Thankfully, everything seemed to be exactly as they left it. Even before he'd climbed down from the wagon, Ben could tell his pride and joy would need extensive work to be usable again.

Harrison dismounted and inspected the stagecoach. He pushed at the supporting brackets and ran his hands over the woodwork. He shook his head sadly. Ben's heart thudded. "Beyond repair?" he asked, his voice shaking. Did he really want to hear the truth?

The other men hurried to unload the remaining luggage. The sooner they got back to town, the better. A storm was brewing. He could feel it. Ben had done more than his fair share of traveling—his stagecoach business saw to that. It meant he'd learned to read the weather, and right now? He wanted to get himself and his friends back to safety.

"It's fixable," Harrison said. "Whether it's worth the effort is another thing. As you can see, much of the frame needs replacing. There are places where the wood has broken right through."

Where they'd hit the rock, no doubt. Ben pulled off his hat and ran a gloved hand through his hair. Was Harrison correct? Was it worth the effort, or the cost involved? He had other stagecoaches, but it would leave him one short if he discarded this one. "I'll need to think on it," he said, sadness now creeping in.

"One thing is for certain," Harrison said. "You need to get it out of the weather or it will be worthless."

Ben knew Harrison was right, but what was he to do about it? He had a large canvas he'd brought to cover the luggage, so perhaps they could make that work. His eyes flicked to the back of the wagon, then to the stagecoach. It might not completely cover the stagecoach, but perhaps it would be enough to ensure it wasn't damaged further. He had plenty of rope, and hopefully between the two, he could save his business. Or at least this coach.

He pulled the canvas down from the wagon with Harrison's help. All the luggage was now on the back of the wagon, and between them, the men covered the stagecoach, then tied it down as best they could.

Ben stared at the coach that was once the pride of his business. Then guilt overtook him. He should be thankful no one was injured in the accident. Instead, only wood and metal were harmed. That was where he needed to place his focus. And his gratitude.

He glanced at the sky again. "Time to go," he shouted above the wind. "Bad weather is moving in." Soon, they were on their way back to Grand Falls.

Chapter Six

Abigail stood at the window watching the snow fall. Snow had always intrigued her. One minute it was light, and the next it could be heavy. She hoped Mr. Diamond and the other men were safe. It seemed foolish to go in this weather, simply to recover luggage.

It wasn't worth a man's life to retrieve possessions. At least, that was her opinion. She startled as Mrs. Baker sidled up beside her. "We're in for a storm," she said. "You mark my words." Who better to know than someone who was born and bred here? "Might even end up being a blizzard."

Abigail turned to face her. "A blizzard? You get those here?" Abigail was surprised at the suggestion. Or perhaps she was scared. Abigail had never been through a blizzard, although she'd heard tales about them.

Mrs. Baker studied her. "Not for a long time. Over a decade ago now, but all the signs are there." She turned away then. "We'll have to wait and see. The water is boiled. Would you like tea?"

Never one to refuse tea, especially on such a chilly day, Abigail accepted. She was about to turn away from the window when she breathed a sigh of relief. "The men are back," she called over her shoulder.

Mrs. Baker turned to face her. "Good," she said, her face appearing more relaxed. She quickly returned carrying a tray laden with two mugs and a plate of sliced pound cake. The aroma was enticing. From all accounts she'd heard so far, Abigail knew the cake would be delicious.

The mug of tea was placed in front of her on the table. She reached out and sipped the hot beverage. "Thank you," Abigail said. "I needed that."

Her hostess studied her. Eyebrows raised, she opened her mouth to speak, then closed it again. She sipped her tea, then placed the mug on the table in front of herself. "Abigail," she said gently, then paused. It was as though she was measuring her words, which likely she was. "I know you don't want to talk about it, dear, but if your safety is at risk…"

Mrs. Baker let her words hang, and Abigail knew she was right. She was more concerned about this dear lady's safety, and that of everyone else in town. She pushed her mug aside, and Mrs. Baker reached for her hands. "I don't know where to start." Abigail took a long, fortifying breath and let it out slowly. "A few months ago, I met a man, Samuel Bosworth. He was lovely, or so it seemed at the time."

Telling her story was both disturbing and beneficial. Apart from the sheriff back in Devil's Edge, Abigail hadn't told another soul. As she finished her story, she felt equally relieved and drained. She glanced at Mrs. Baker. Her lips were in a tight line—it was obvious she was not pleased. Abigail was disappointed. Mrs. Baker was angry because she'd kept the information from her.

"How dare he!" she suddenly bellowed. This quiet spoken woman who never said a word out of place was bellowing. It certainly surprised Abigail. She also felt relief since she now understood her hostess was not angry at her, but her captor. "I will speak to our sheriff. He is good in these matters." Mrs. Baker straightened her back as if in determination.

"I don't think…" She didn't get to finish the sentence. Mrs. Baker was already on her feet and pulling on her coat and gloves.

"Come along. Your boots should be dry now." She handed Abigail her coat. There was no option but to comply.

Sheriff Earl Saxon was certainly a cut above the previous sheriff she'd dealt with. He was attentive, took notes, and vowed to ensure her safety. Not that anyone thought Samuel Bosworth could find her. Even that was dependent on the weather. He'd need to travel from town to town asking about her. Surely someone would become suspicious?

Leaving Sheriff Saxon's office, Abigail felt relieved. At least now she knew the law was aware of the situation and would look out for her. And for Samuel. She had thought Samuel unhinged, and the sheriff here in Grand Falls believed the same. He promised to alert other lawmen to be on the lookout. They had no image of her kidnapper, which wasn't at all helpful.

She was lucky to get away unharmed. Abigail was already convinced of it, but Sheriff Saxon had reiterated the fact. Her heart pounded. She really was blessed. Who knew what Samuel might have done to her? The fact she'd escaped unscathed was a miracle, and she knew it.

"Good morning." Benjamin Diamond waved as he greeted them from outside the diner. Then he frowned. Had he noticed they were leaving the sheriff's office? Abigail hoped to keep her secret exactly that—secret. She'd already been warned nothing was private in a small town such as this one. She was discovering for herself it was true.

"Mr. Diamond," her companion said as they crossed the road toward him.

Without another word, he opened the door to the diner and ushered the pair inside. "It's warmer in here," he said, and quickly closed the door behind them. He guided them to a table beside the fire. "We managed to retrieve everyone's luggage," he said, but didn't elaborate.

"What about your stagecoach?" Abigail asked, trepidation in her question. She hoped it wasn't beyond repair.

"Unfortunately, it doesn't look great," he said. "The good news is, no one was injured." Tucker headed toward their table. "All thanks to Tucker and the others who came along to help."

Moments later, Sheriff Saxon strode through the door, followed by a barrage of snow. He slammed the door closed, then headed straight for Abigail. Not waiting for an invitation, he sat at their table. "I've had a telegraph. There's a blizzard headed this way. Bosworth is unlikely to get through."

Abigail's heart pounded. She was pleased Samuel couldn't get to her, but now she was stuck here? She felt guilty at even thinking such a thing. The people of Grand Falls were lovely. Not one person had been horrid or unfriendly. She thanked her lucky stars she had landed here and not somewhere else. Who knows where she would be right now?

Tucker had been hovering until that moment. Then he hurried away, returning soon afterwards with mugs of coffee and tea for all.

"I'm glad we could secure the wreckage," Benjamin said. "How long before the blizzard hits?"

Sheriff Saxon scratched his chin. "Hard to say. Perhaps a day, possibly more."

Tucker gulped his coffee. "I remember the last blizzard, even though I was a young boy." He drank down another mouthful of the hot beverage. "From what I recall, it wasn't fun. My father secured all the horses and locked down all the equipment. We lost a couple of wagons, and the office had to be rebuilt afterwards."

It sounded terrible, and Abigail was feeling afraid. On the other hand, it would mean Samuel Bosworth could not travel to find her. Wouldn't it?

Benjamin Diamond glanced her way. "You've gone deathly white, Miss Brooks," he said, concern in his expression. Abigail glanced down at the mug of tea in her shaking hands. Tea spilled over the sides. His hands suddenly covered hers. "What can I do to help?" he whispered.

Abigail wasn't sure what to say. Was she more afraid of the blizzard or of her kidnapper? She had to admit her captor scared her far more than any snow storm, even if that storm eventually turned into a blizzard.

Mrs. Baker reached over and touched her shoulder. It was comforting, but not as reassuring as Benjamin's touch. Her thoughts sent heat curling up to her cheeks.

The mug was slowly brought to the table, and he let his hands drop away. The loss of Benjamin's touch was great. Abigail couldn't understand the reason. Benjamin Diamond was a stranger. They'd known each other less than twenty-four hours, and yet, his touch affected her like no other.

She shivered when she thought about the way Samuel Bosworth had tried to touch her. Abigail had shied away, and he'd let it go. If she'd stayed even another day or two, who knew what might have happened? He had convinced himself they were married. That alone told her the man was unhinged.

Mrs. Baker leaned in close and whispered in her ear. "You should tell him," she said, ensuring no one else could hear. Abigail nodded, but wasn't certain it was the right thing to do. The more people who knew meant those townsfolk were in danger.

Abigail glanced around the table. These were all good people. Tucker, Benjamin, and Sheriff Saxon. Not to mention her wonderful hostess. She opened her mouth to speak, but the words wouldn't come.

"Would you like me to do the honors, dear?" Mrs. Baker asked, her expression one of understanding.

Abigail nodded again. It seemed like it was all she was capable of right now. The older woman reached over and covered her hand. "Abigail is in danger," Mrs. Baker said, and Abigail heard the collected gasp that went around the table. "Sheriff Saxon, would you like to tell them?"

"Of course," the sheriff said, then laid out the details of what had occurred. The men listened carefully. Abigail watched as fury covered Benjamin's face. "I doubt he can get through the storm. But we need to be on the lookout."

The stagecoach driver slid his hand across the table and covered Abigail's. "I will look after you," he said firmly. "Mrs. Baker, I will stay at your place until we know Miss Brooks is safe." His eyes pierced both women, and Abigail could see his determination. She'd seen the same expression on her attacker when he'd first abducted her. At least this time, she knew no harm would come to her.

"I don't have a spare bed," the older woman told him. "You are welcome to stay, though. I can make up a pallet for you."

Abigail listened as everyone made decisions about her. Who would look out for her, and how they would go about it. Not once did they consult her about her feelings. "I don't want to put anyone else in danger," she said, shoving the chair back as she stood. Hurrying to the door, she grabbed her coat and gloves, then ran outside.

She was certain they were all trying to help, but why didn't anyone ask her what she thought?

Abigail hurried along the boardwalk. Heavy footsteps behind her quickly caught up, and a hand reached out and grabbed her around the waist. Abigail gasped.

Chapter Seven

Ben hastened his pace to catch up with Abigail. She'd taken him by surprise when she'd run out of the diner. It would have been a full half minute, if not longer, before he'd moved. Her story had caught him off guard.

Why would anyone want to kidnap her? From what the sheriff said, the man had to be unbalanced. Why else would he lock Abigail away from everyone? From all accounts, she was lucky to escape with her life.

As he reached out to stop her running further, and perhaps into danger, he hadn't thought. The moment his arm snaked around her waist, she gasped. Her hands pounded his arm, and she struggled to get away. "Abigail," he said urgently. "It's me, Ben." He heard her breath leaving her lips, and she sagged against him. "I apologize. I obviously didn't think it through."

She reached up and swiped at her eyes. He'd made her cry. Guilt engulfed him. Why on earth hadn't he thought about what he was doing? Of course, she was scared. She'd already endured one life-changing event, and his actions were deplorable. Especially given he knew what she'd been through recently.

He spun her around in his arms. "I truly am sorry," he said gently. "What a fool I am. I should have known better." She stared into his face, and he wanted to crawl into a hole in the ground. She swiped a hand across her face again. Ben lifted a hand and wiped away her tears. Abigail tried to turn away. He understood. She felt embarrassed, and didn't want him to see her so... emotional.

"You gave me a fright, that's all," she said firmly. "I want to look around town."

He stared at her curiously. "For what reason?" He was more than a little confused. Why would she want to do such a thing?

Abigail swallowed, then licked her lips. "I need to know where I can hide if necessary," she said, her eyes never leaving his.

His heart thudded. She really thought her abductor was coming after her. No wonder she'd kept to herself most of the time. Abigail didn't know who she could trust. "I'll take care of you, I promise," he said, pulling her close against himself. Ben knew he shouldn't do it—he had no rights to her, and propriety said he mustn't. But he liked it. From the expression on Abigail's face, she enjoyed it, too.

Mrs. Baker's image danced before his eyes. The woman was relentless and would hunt him down if he ruined Abigail's reputation. "I can show you around town," he told her. "Although you won't need a place to hide. I *will* look after you. There won't be a moment you are alone and unprotected."

He felt her stiffen in his arms. "It's not your job," she whispered against his chest. His arms had a mind of their own, and without his permission, came up around her back. From this day forth, until she no longer needed his protection, he would spend every waking moment with Abigail Brooks.

The thought of what happened afterwards truly bothered him.

Ben heard the diner door open momentarily, then close. His friends were checking up on them. He was certain it was true. As far as everyone knew, Abigail's abductor was not in town. If it meant she felt more comfortable, or even safer, he would show her around. Then perhaps she wouldn't be so flighty.

"Are you warm enough?" he asked. "We'll go now."

"Where are we going?" she asked, her wariness clear to hear.

He flicked snow from her collar and stared into her eyes. "I'll show you around town. You won't need it, but it's obvious you'll feel more secure knowing where everything is located."

She nodded then. Ben offered her his arm, and she hooked her arm through his. Then they began the tour of Grand Falls, such as it was. The town was small compared to many of the towns surrounding them. There was a small main road, then an alley connecting a side road that housed a few more businesses. The men's boarding house was down an alleyway that ran along the side of the main road. He showed her all these places.

He warned the alleyway running behind the main road was particularly dark at night, and while it might seem like a good place to hide, it really wasn't. Apart from the back entrance to some of the stores, there was nowhere she could run.

When the tour was over, he turned to her. "This is all moot, anyway. As I said, I will keep you safe. I'll be by your side every waking moment. I'll sleep near the front door to Mrs. Baker's house, and if anyone tries to enter, I will stop them."

Abigail frowned. "I can't ask you…"

He held up a hand to stop her words. "You didn't ask, I offered. I have been protecting my stagecoach from robbers for years. I know how to handle a gun, and how to handle myself." It was true. He'd only needed to use his firearm a few times, but he was more than proficient. He'd made certain of it before his first stagecoach run.

Here in Grand Falls, no one expected they'd need to be armed, but most folks still were. With the snow the way it was, and the threat of a blizzard, their guard might be down. Ben had no intention of letting that happen in this case.

Abigail Brooks deserved better. She needed protection, and Ben would ensure she received it. "I hate to ask, Miss Brooks, but do you own a gun?" Her eyes opened wide in astonishment.

"I… no, I don't," she said, her voice incredulous. "Do I need one?"

He guided her toward the gun store. "I'd rather be careful than be sorry," he said, then led her inside. They went straight to the front counter. "Mornin' Cecil," Ben said. "We're looking for a small gun for my friend." He'd had dealings with the store owner in the past, but didn't know the man well. The less information he knew, the better.

Never one to say much unless it mattered, Cecil nodded. He turned his back to them and reached up to retrieve some firearms from the small display on the wall. "This here Derringer is the one I recommend," Cecil said. "They fit nicely in the pockets of the ladies' skirts." He handed the firearm to Ben.

Abigail stared at him, her eyes wide and wild. It was clear she had not used guns and clearly had no wish to do so. He checked the chamber to ensure the gun wasn't loaded, then held it in his hands as if to fire it. The gun was tiny in his hands, but would be perfect for a woman as small as Abigail. "How effective is it?" he asked Cecil.

"It packs a punch," he said, then turned away, leaving them alone momentarily. He glanced at Abigail. It was clear she was uncomfortable with this turn of events, but it was beyond his control. She needed to be armed—there was no compromise.

He stood behind her, then reached for her hands. "Hold this," he whispered. The tremor of her hands told him all he needed to know. She was terrified to even touch it. He placed the Derringer in her hands, then closed his hands over hers, forcing her to hold it. Her hands still shaking, he removed it from her grip. "Take off your gloves," he demanded. "You need to feel it. To know exactly what it feels like against your skin."

She turned her head and stared at him with sad eyes, but didn't protest. It was all he could ask. He pulled his gloves off too, and the small gun felt completely different. He knew it would, and it was the very reason he insisted she do the same. As he stood behind her, his arms against hers, her body next to him, and their hands skin to skin, Ben knew his life had changed forever.

For now, though, he vowed to protect her, and protect Abigail he would.

Chapter Eight

Abigail stood, feet apart, heart pounding, facing the cans Benjamin had set up. Loaded Derringer in her hands, she was shaking far more than she'd ever endured before. He stood beside her, a short distance away, and watched her every move.

The pistol shook in time with her hands. This was not her first attempt, and yet she still trembled.

"It won't harm you," Benjamin said gently. His hands swiftly covered hers. "What we want is for you to be proficient enough to harm an attacker." Benjamin's firm grip stopped her hands shaking, but her heart continued to pound. For an entirely different reason.

"I…" She shook her head. "I don't think I can do this." His eyes showed the sadness he was feeling about the entire situation. She'd caused his misery. If she hadn't been on his stagecoach, none of this would be affecting him. "Forget about me," Abigail said firmly. "You have better things to do."

He scowled then. "There is nothing else for me to do. My stagecoach is laying on its side, and the weather has turned nasty. If my barn was full with the stagecoach, we couldn't practice. Since we can, let's make the most of it. Once the weather clears, that will change."

Abigail sighed, and he moved closer. As much as she liked it when he was close to her, Abigail knew it was not the best thing for either of them. Once the blizzard hit, and then was over, they would go their separate ways. She was becoming far too comfortable with Benjamin Diamond. It seemed he also was comfortable with her. It really had to stop, but Benjamin was right—she needed to be capable of defending herself.

True to his promise, he'd moved into Mrs. Baker's cottage, where a pallet was set up near the door for him. It was clear their hostess was enjoying his company, but Abigail had suspected there was far more to it. Benjamin warned her Mrs. Baker liked to play the matchmaker, and usually won. Neither of them were interested in marriage, so they went along with her to keep Mrs. Baker off their backs. Now she wondered if that had been a mistake.

They'd practiced several times today, as well as the previous day, but still she was fearful of the small pistol in her hands. Without warning, he took it from her hands. He unloaded it, placing the bullets in his pocket. "It is no longer a danger to you. Hold it. Feel the shape of it."

She frowned. What was he playing at? This was the absolute opposite of what he'd been trying to get her to do. He handed the Derringer back and sat it on her palm. Abigail gazed at it.

Benjamin closed his hand over hers, causing her to shudder. He stared down at her, daring her to hold it by herself. She was certain of it. Abigail straightened her shoulders and pulled her hands out of his gentle grip. She ran her hands over the offending item, trying not to shiver, then lifted her hands and held it the way Benjamin had showed her.

"That's good," he said, his voice holding a hint of pleasure. "Now let's try it loaded."

Abigail didn't want to do this. Instead, she wanted to leave Grand Falls and find somewhere else to hide. Unfortunately, there was no way out. Even the trains couldn't get through with this horrific weather. Benjamin must realize she didn't enjoy using a gun. She'd never liked firearms, but secretly she wished she'd had a gun when she was kidnapped. She may have been able to escape sooner.

It made her wonder if she could even shoot a man when it came down to it. Clearly she had trouble shooting cans, so if her life was in danger, could she do it? Would she do it?

Benjamin handed her the ammunition. She stared at him. Abigail had never loaded a gun before. "It's easy," he said before she spoke even a word, then showed her exactly what to do. He was right, it was easy. "Just don't point the thing at anyone unless you intend to shoot them." Abigail didn't answer. Of course, she wouldn't shoot anyone. It wasn't in her nature to do so. Benjamin reached out and put his fingers to her chin. He turned her to face him. "Promise me, if the need arises, you *will* shoot."

She swallowed. How could she promise such a thing when she had no idea if she could fulfill that promise?

Benjamin dropped his hand, then moved behind her. His arms next to hers, he covered her hands as she readied herself to shoot the cans at the other end of the barn. "Aim for the one in the middle," he said firmly. "Then pull the trigger."

She hesitated for only a moment. With Benjamin there to support her, Abigail felt far more confident than she would have been alone. She pulled the trigger and missed the can altogether. Disappointment filled her. "I can't do this," she told him firmly.

"Yes, you can. You must. Now try again."

They continued until Abigail hit one can. It might not have been the one she was aiming for, but she hit something.

"Better, but not good enough," Benjamin told her. "We'll take a break, then come back and practice again. If you need to shoot someone, you *must* be able to hit them. Missing could mean the end of your life."

Abigail felt lightheaded. She knew he was right, but that didn't mean he had to say the words out loud. She turned to face him. "I know you're trying to help, but I really don't think I can do this." She knew she sounded like a spoiled rich kid, but she was only telling the truth.

Benjamin frowned. "I will not accept that. You must do it. Your life depends on it." He took the gun from her hands and unloaded it. "Put it in your pocket. Get used to the feel of it there. From now on, it will be your constant companion. Right now it's unloaded. Soon it will have ammunition in it wherever you go." She opened her mouth to protest, but he put up a hand. "No arguments. I don't want to find you lying dead somewhere. This gun is your only means of protection if something happens to me."

Was he expecting to be killed? Because of her? Abigail couldn't bear the thought. Tears sprung into her eyes and rolled down her cheeks. For his sake, she needed to do this. When they returned, she would show him how capable she was.

Abigail was more determined than ever.

Abigail sat at Mrs. Baker's dining table, decidedly uncomfortable.

She was fully aware of the Derringer sitting in her skirt pocket, and wanted to reach in and toss it out. There was only one reason she didn't, and that was Benjamin Diamond sitting beside her. Her saving grace was Benjamin held the ammunition in *his* pocket. They both knew she needed to assert herself further if this was to work. Her aversion to firearms was holding Abigail back. That was not her fault, and it certainly wasn't Benjamin's. It stemmed back to her childhood when her father accidentally shot her pet dog. Jock never harmed a soul, and didn't deserve to be shot. He ran out in front of Father while he was hunting for rabbits. It had been a painful time in her young life, but she'd never got over the memory of that day.

As she ate, Abigail lamented the day's activities. Benjamin was a big man, strong and handsome, too. When he touched her, a shiver ran down her spine. Sitting near to him was no different. Something had changed the moment he touched her. He might have been trying to protect her, as well as comfort her the day she fled from the diner, but he'd unknowingly done far more.

"This pot roast is delicious, Mrs. Baker," Benjamin said.

Abigail had to agree. "It truly is. I can honestly say it's the best meal I've ever had."

Mrs. Baker turned to face her. "Thank you both," she said as she faced Abigail. Did she not believe her? Becoming an orphan at fifteen, she'd missed being sent to an orphanage by the skin of her teeth. Since then, she'd drifted from town to town, getting whatever work she could. There was never a lot of money, and especially not to buy food at the diner. This simple meal, as Mrs. Baker had described it earlier, was more like a feast to Abigail. She'd never starved, but she'd never eaten as well as she had since arriving in this wonderful little town. More's the pity she would soon be leaving.

"How did you do today?" Mrs. Baker asked, still studying her.

Abigail scowled. "Not very good. We're going back after our meal. I need to do better."

"You will, I know you will. It all takes practice," the older woman told her. "It's a pity we don't have a photograph. You could practice shooting his face!" At first Abigail thought she was joking, but when she glanced across, Mrs. Baker was dead serious. "Men like that don't deserve to live. Don't you agree, Mr. Diamond?"

He smiled tentatively. "I prefer to see them rot in jail for the rest of their lives," he said, glancing at Abigail. "Killing them is the easy way out—for them." Abigail totally agreed.

Chapter Nine

Ben handed her the bullets. "Load the gun, then shoot." He stood back and watched. He wanted to work out why she wasn't shooting straight. That was difficult to determine standing behind her.

Abigail pulled the Derringer from her pocket. She was still hesitant about handling it. Heck, she was uncertain she even wanted it in her pocket. Ben felt for her. He really did, but her very existence was at stake.

Who knew what this Samuel Bosworth was capable of? It was clear Abigail wasn't or she wouldn't have gone anywhere with the man. The fact she'd escaped was a miracle. God had been looking out for her.

"Put your feet slightly apart. It will help steady you." Abigail did what he suggested. She fired off one bullet. This time she didn't flinch backwards as she had before. Already an improvement. "I noticed your arms are slightly bent. Try keeping them perfectly straight. And keep your eyes on the target."

"It's hard to tell which one I am to shoot," she said, dismay in her voice.

That was easy to fix. "Lower the gun. I'm going to make some adjustments." Ben strolled down to the pile of cans sitting at the end of the barn. Instead of having them all crammed together, he separated them. Now they were five or six inches apart. "Better?" he called to her.

Abigail studied the new setup. "I'm not sure yet, but perhaps. It certainly makes it easier to see which one I'm to shoot at."

"You won't have that problem when it's Samuel Bosworth you're aiming for," Ben said as he approached her. "Try again now." He stood beside her and watched her stance. Everything seemed fine now, and if they could perfect her technique, that tin can should be destroyed, even if she was using a Derringer. Abigail glanced at him, then turned toward the cans Ben had placed on the table at the far end of the barn. "Pretend it's your abductor you're shooting at. He is about to lock you away in that house."

Ben watched as fury rose in her cheeks. They'd gone from ghostly white to bright red. His well-chosen words had worked. Now to see if she could hit the target.

The sound of the bullet firing echoed in the near empty barn. The ping when it hit the can was even louder. Ben watched in amazement as the bullet connected with the tin can and knocked it off the table.

Abigail squealed. "Did I really do that?" She did a little dance, she was so excited.

He took the gun from her hands. Ben had no intention of being the next recipient of a bullet. "Safety first, Abigail," he said when she frowned.

She nodded solemnly. "I apologize. I didn't think." Suddenly, she wrapped her arms around him. "Thank you for having confidence in me. Without you, I couldn't have done this."

Ben reveled in the feel of her arms around him. He wanted to pull her closer, but knew he shouldn't. If he gave into his feelings, who knew where it would lead them? His only focus now was to ensure Abigail could shoot an attacker. Reluctantly, he pushed her away. "Ready to try again? This time, aim for the can on the left." He handed her the gun and watched her prepare to shoot.

She lifted the gun and turned her body sideways, then pulled the trigger. Another tin can fell to the ground. Two in a row—it could still be a fluke. She turned to face him, a smile on her face. "How was that?" she asked, obviously pleased with herself.

"That was good. You'll need to reload now. Can you hit the last tin can on the right?" Samuel Bosworth would not be a static target and that would be the problem, but if Abigail's confidence was lifted, she might not think too much about that.

She loaded two more bullets, turned to face her target, then pulled the trigger. Another tin can hit the ground. She beamed. Ben grinned. Now he knew she could shoot and hit the target, they would have to practice with a moving target, but he didn't want to get ahead of himself.

"Wonderful," he said. "The problem with the Derringer is you only have two bullets. It will get you out of a scrape, don't get me wrong."

She stared down at the small pistol in her hand. "It's easy to conceal. There's no doubt about that." Abigail continued to study the Derringer. "What if I miss him in two shots?" She swallowed, and Ben knew she understood the consequences.

"What if you don't?" he whispered.

It was then Ben heard shuffling behind them, and turned, his hand on his holster.

"How is it going?" Mrs. Baker asked. "I heard shots, and then I didn't."

"I hit my target three times," Abigail told her, excitement still clear in her voice.

Mrs. Baker glanced at Ben. "You did well, my dear," she said, then pierced Ben with her eyes. He knew what she was thinking—the same thing he had thought earlier. A tin can differed totally from a moving target. How he was going to replicate a man running toward her, he did not know. The last thing he wanted to do was leave it to fate. They were dealing with a life or death situation, and Abigail needed to be prepared for any consequence.

"We've been invited to afternoon tea at the diner. I expect everyone would like an update."

Ben would never refuse good food and even better coffee. "I believe Abigail could do with a break about now," he said, and watched as Abigail removed the last bullet from the chamber. She handed it over to him, and he put it in his pocket.

He would ponder the problem of only two bullets. Hitting a tin can was one thing. Being confronted by a gun wielding man was another situation entirely. The Derringer was perfect for a lady, provided she was not being abducted by a crazy person. Who knew what the man was capable of? That was the risk they were taking with such a pistol.

Ben's hand slid from the top to the bottom of his own gun. The one he wore on the stagecoach for protection. He also had a rifle under the seat. Abigail would have no such luxury.

Mrs. Baker's eyes watched his every move. He almost missed the tiny nod she sent his way. The woman was incredible—she understood far more than people gave her credit for. She might be old, but she was not stupid.

"I'm sure you both deserve a break," Mrs. Baker said, hooking her arm through Abigail's. "I'm looking forward to whatever Mr. Smith is serving up this afternoon. He has a new cook, so that could be interesting." She smiled then, and Ben wondered what she was up to. Mrs. Baker always had some new scheme going on. It was quite some time since she signed the diner over to Tucker and his wife. The woman had to fill her days somehow. If scheming did it for her, so be it.

Chapter Ten

Abigail sat next to the fire, Ben on one side of her, and Mrs. Baker on the other. With everything that had happened recently, she'd forgotten it was almost Christmas. Her only clue was the Christmas decorations, which had appeared since she was last in the diner.

There was a string of paper angels hanging above the fireplace, and each table had a Christmas centerpiece. A box of other decorations sat on a table close to theirs. Tucker hurried over with a tray full of beverages and a plate full of assorted muffins. He handed them out to his guests. "Tea or coffee, Abigail?" he asked.

"Tea, thank you," she said, then took a sip the moment it hit the table. Abigail couldn't get over the people of Grand Falls. Not only did they offer hospitality to each of the stranded passengers, but also friendship. She felt overwhelmed by it.

She glanced up as the diner door opened. Abigail felt warmth fill her as Maisy and Gertrude strolled in. They hurried over when they noticed her. "Oh, my dear girl," Maisy said, then hugged her so tight, Abigail could barely breathe.

"It's so good to see you both," Abigail said once Maisy released her.

Gertrude moved in and hugged her, but wasn't so aggressive with her embrace. "How are you faring?" Gertrude asked, then slid into a chair at their table. Maisy followed suit.

Abigail had no intention of telling the sisters her troubles. They didn't seem worldly, and she worried her dire situation would distress them. "Mrs. Baker is looking after me far better than anyone could expect," she said instead. It wasn't an untruth—her hostess had been wonderful. "And you?" she asked, assuming they would receive similar treatment.

"Mr. Davis and his wife are caring for us wonderfully," Maisy said. "We really appreciate their hospitality." She turned to Gertrude. "Isn't that right, Sister?"

Gertrude nodded. "They certainly are. Our treatment here cannot be faulted." She turned to Benjamin then. "Did you manage to repair your stagecoach, Mr. Diamond?" she asked.

It was clear to Abigail the sisters were very close. She wondered if the pair lived together or were merely traveling together. She would probably never know.

"Help yourselves to muffins," Tucker told the older ladies, as he placed a mug of hot liquid in front of each sister.

As they drank and ate, everyone chatted. Abigail felt as though she had known these people for years, when in fact it was mere days. She shifted on her chair, then remembered the firearm she carried in her skirt pocket. It put a damper on an otherwise pleasant afternoon.

Once the pleasantries were over and everyone dispersed, Benjamin told Abigail it was time to practice once more. She was happy to spend time with him, but had a feeling of impending doom.

When he stood, then helped Abigail to her feet, her heart thudded. His jacket opened, and she spotted the gun that was previously hidden from view. Again, she felt fear overtake her. The Colt sitting undisturbed in his holster both bothered and reassured her.

Seeing it there made her wonder if her comparably small Derringer would be effective. She would ask Benjamin when they returned to the barn.

"I thought a stroll around town before we begin practice again would be nice," he told her.

Abigail pulled her collar up around her neck. Two teenagers were shoveling snow on the boardwalk, which helped tremendously. Otherwise, she would have wet boots again, and Abigail knew she would be stuck inside waiting for them to dry. "There's an icy chill in the air, but you're right, it is pleasant," she told him. They'd already spent several hours today practicing her shooting skills. Abigail wasn't sure how, but knew if there was a way to get to her, Samuel would find one.

She glanced about the main street, reassuring herself he wasn't there. Benjamin's hand went to her back. "He's not here," he whispered. "Sheriff Saxon is on the lookout, along with several of the town's men. He won't get to you."

Abigail closed her eyes momentarily. Benjamin Diamond seemed to read her thoughts. Otherwise, how did he know what she was thinking?

"I know what it's like to be on the lookout, to check if anyone is there who shouldn't be. It can be frightening." Of course he knew. Riding the stagecoach, watching for outlaws couldn't be fun. In fact, it was surely terrifying. "We need to be vigilant all the time. It's exhausting. I know from personal experience." His arm went up around her shoulders then, and Abigail felt better. Protected. Although now she knew she could shoot straight, and it was more likely she would hit her target.

"Is… is the Derringer big enough?" she asked out of the blue, surprising even herself. Benjamin appeared to be taken off guard.

"I had the same thought," he said. "If you hit your target, it will be fine. If you don't, you only have one more chance."

Abigail gasped, then swallowed. She would not let this revelation scare her. "Mr. Diamond," she said. "Should I use a larger gun?" Her voice sounded strange to her own ears.

He stared at her. Not in a surprised way, but as though he was expecting it. "Call me Ben. Everyone does. I have been considering introducing you to a larger firearm. The only disadvantage is you won't be able to conceal it."

Abigail studied him. Feeling his gaze burn into her soul, she turned away, glancing over his shoulder instead. "Of that, I am not concerned. If it means wearing a holster on my waist, so be it." She felt more emboldened not gazing into his face. Now, though, her heart thudded with trepidation. She wasn't so sure now her words were out in the open.

A grin slowly covered his face. "You really are something, Abigail Brooks. You know that?" His grin turned to a laugh, and she couldn't help but join in, whether he was laughing at her, or with her. Ben reached into his pocket and pulled out a handful of bullets. "While you are feeling so inspired, load your Derringer, and leave the spare bullets in your pocket. Get used to the weight."

She held out her hand. It was shaking. Had she spoken too soon? Only time would tell.

It was warmer in the barn, not a lot, but not having snow fall on and around her was a bonus. Ben handed her his gun after unloading the chamber. "The Colt is a far bigger gun, meant for a man's larger hands."

Abigail laid it across her palm, much as Ben had done when he'd first given her the Derringer. Her heart thudded—it seemed to be almost constant now, but she was getting used to it. She ran her fingers along the barrel and caressed it, almost as if it was a lover.

This gun, or one like it, could be her saving grace. Her lifesaver. Abigail was no longer convinced the Derringer would be. With only two bullets in the chamber, if Samuel rushed at her and she missed, where would she be then?

Seven rounds in the chamber gave her a better than remote chance of surviving. She wrapped her fingers around the handle. Ben's Colt was a practical gun. One meant to maim or kill.

A shudder went through her, but Abigail knew in her heart that Samuel wouldn't hesitate to shoot her.

She'd escaped and spoiled all his plans. She wasn't sure what he'd had in mind for her, but she had ruined it for him, and she doubted he would be happy.

Abigail closed her eyes momentarily and took a long, fortifying breath. She could do this, she must do it. Or die.

Chapter Eleven

Ben watched Abigail caress his Colt. He didn't miss her initial reluctance, but she now seemed determined to excel in this endeavor.

Her fingers roaming over his gun were almost his undoing. He would like nothing more than to pull her close and kiss her senseless, but knew he couldn't succumb to his wanton feelings. Whether it was because they'd spent the past days in close proximity, he wasn't sure, but knew he must keep his distance.

A relationship was not something he was interested in. Not until now anyway, but the subject of his feelings was in danger and he couldn't let anything inhibit him from protecting her.

"Can I have the bullets?" Abigail's demand alerted him to her readiness. He still wasn't certain about this, but if it was what she wanted, he wouldn't quell her eagerness. Not unless he deemed it too much for her.

"If you're certain," he began, but she interrupted him.

Palm up, she waited. "Bullets," she demanded again, and a shudder went through him at her determination.

After loading the Colt, she steadied herself. Feet slightly apart, she held the firearm in both hands. Then she pulled the trigger.

Abigail's entire body jolted backwards from the recoil, and he noticed her surprise at this turn of events. He should have warned her, but worried she would have changed her mind. Instead, she turned to him and smiled. "I hit it," she said, raising her eyebrows. "There's little chance I would miss with one of these."

The glee on her face worried him. Would she shoot Samuel Bosworth without hesitation if he came to town?

"You did well," Ben said, not wanting to appear too enthusiastic. His concern was not the size of the firearm, but more the confidence it seemed to impart. If Abigail believed she could stop her abductor with a larger firearm, would she shoot without giving him a chance? Would she even give him the opportunity to declare he'd done the wrong thing by her?

He couldn't answer either of those questions, but had to ensure she was ready if he came for her.

Abigail turned and smiled at him. "I did, didn't I?"

Ben's heart thudded. It was as he feared—she was becoming far too confident. Not that it was necessarily a bad thing. It was certainly better than her feeling incompetent with a gun in her hand. Every woman needed to be able to defend herself when required, and in this case, Abigail was convinced Samuel Bosworth would come after her. They hadn't known each other for long, but it was long enough for Ben to know he was falling for Abigail. He suddenly understood why the other man wanted her close to him, but he must surely be deranged to kidnap any woman and call her his wife.

And therein was the problem. If they were dealing with a man who was sane and had his wits about him, there would be no issue. But this man was clearly unhinged and would not be one to negotiate with.

The mere thought of it bothered Ben beyond comprehension. Add to that, he didn't know what the other man looked like, and he had a predicament. People came and left Grand Falls. Many stayed long term, but every week a handful of strangers passed through. In particular, traveling salesmen. How would he determine which of these people was Samuel Bosworth? The last thing he wanted to do was have Abigail confirm her attacker. If the kidnapper saw her, it may put Abigail in further danger.

"Ben?"

Abigail's sweet voice broke through his musings. He turned to face her. "You did. I'll set it up again for you," he said. He couldn't help but worry—what if Bosworth sneaked into town despite the snow and pending blizzard? Could any man be so determined to claim a woman as his own?

As he reset the cans at the end of the barn, Ben knew he had to come up with some kind of plan. He would speak with the sheriff later, after Abigail had become more used to his Colt. A visit to the gun shop was also in order—to get himself a new Colt. He'd leave his gun with Abigail since she was now familiar with it. The fewer distractions the better.

He would fulfill his promise to both Abigail and Mrs. Baker, and ensure Abigail was safe.

Mrs. Baker opened the door to her cottage, and the aroma of food baking hit him.

"How did you do, my dear?" Mrs. Baker asked, holding the door open.

"She did well. Abigail mastered using the Colt today." Mrs. Baker frowned. He did not want the wrath of the older lady and decided to deflect the subject. "What are you baking? It smells delicious."

Her face brightened. "I've begun my Christmas baking. I have a fruitcake in the oven. The spices fill the house and make me feel as though Christmas has already arrived."

Ben breathed a sigh of relief. It appeared he'd distracted her away from the subject of Abigail handling his Colt.

"Firing a Colt is completely different from a Derringer," she told Abigail out of the blue.

He should have known better. Mrs. Baker was sharp as a tack. Nothing got past her, and she was always on the ball. Without warning, she reached into the pocket of her skirt. She soon held a Derringer in her tiny hand. "It might not kill someone, but it will certainly stop a man in his tracks. Are you certain you want to handle a bigger gun?"

Abigail's jaw dropped. If he was honest with himself, Ben was shocked at the revelation. Who knew this unassuming elderly woman was toting a firearm in her skirts?

But wasn't that the entire idea? To be armed and ready, and take any attacker off guard?

"Mrs. Baker!" Abigail declared. "I did not know you carried a gun." She blinked twice, as if trying to take in this startling piece of information.

"The element of surprise, my dear. It can do a lot. For me, this small gun has ensured I felt safe living here alone. It hides in my skirt pocket during the day, and under my pillow at night." She placed the small gun back in her pocket. "I suggest you do the same. Now," she said, as though dismissing them both. "I must get back to my baking. Would you like to join me, Miss Brooks?"

Mrs. Baker headed to the kitchen. Abigail stared at Ben for several moments, then followed her hostess.

Chapter Twelve

Abigail was stunned at the news her hostess carried a gun with her.

Mrs. Baker was feisty, she would give her that. She was also a tiny woman of around five feet. There was no doubt in Abigail's mind she would use the firearm if the situation presented itself.

"Do you know how to bake?" The words pulled Abigail out of her musings. Of course, she'd been invited into the kitchen to help Mrs. Baker. Perhaps even to take her mind off her problems. She had no issue with that. These past days had been intense. She'd dealt with a headache for most of the time, and Abigail knew it was due to stress. She had no doubt about it.

"I can bake simple recipes, but haven't done much. Hopefully, the little skill I have in the kitchen will be useful to you."

Mrs. Baker rattled trays then turned to Abigail. "Every woman needs to know how to get around a kitchen. When you marry, your husband will expect well-made home-cooked meals. Not to mention cakes and cookies."

Abigail knew she was right, but she had no wish to marry. At least not right now. Not after her dreadful experience with Samuel.

She glanced down as she rubbed at her ring finger. How did she not realize she was still wearing the ring he'd given her? Abigail wondered if Ben had noticed, and had refrained from mentioning it.

She wrenched the offending ring from her finger and was about to throw it in the trash. "Don't do that," Mrs. Baker told her. "You need to face the man and hand the ring back to him." She stared at Abigail, perhaps waiting for a challenge.

"I understand, but don't want to wear it," Abigail said firmly.

Rummaging through a drawer, Mrs. Baker pulled out a small square of brown paper. "Wrap it in this, and put it in your reticule. Then, when he's here, and I have no doubt he will eventually turn up," she said guardedly, "you can hand it back to him."

Mrs. Baker was right. Samuel Bosworth seemed resolved to claim her as his own. To that end, he would hunt her down like prey. Kidnapping Abigail, and locking her away, had proven his motives and his determination. "Thank you," Abigail said, reaching for the small piece of paper.

Mrs. Baker wrapped her small hand around Abigail's. "Please," she almost begged. "Be careful. Stick close to Mr. Diamond and listen to what he tells you." Tears swam in her eyes, which was confusing. Mrs. Baker didn't seem the sort of woman to break down easily.

"I will, I promise," Abigail whispered. She squeezed the other woman's hand, then carefully wrapped the ring. "I'll place this in my reticule and will be back."

Her heart thudded as she hurried to carry out the small task, and then return to the well-appointed kitchen. Abigail knew Mrs. Baker was right. Samuel would not let his grip on her go that easily. Any man who would kidnap a woman to ensure she married him was not normal.

The fact she hadn't noticed how unhinged he was bothered her. In addition, she worried he would be furious about her escape. Praise the Lord for the people of Grand Falls. Without them, she could be in the clutches of her former fiancé right now. If he got his hands on her again, what would he do?

Abigail wondered if he still wanted her, or whether Samuel Bosworth would be out for revenge.

Mrs. Baker stood back and studied the rewards of their baking efforts. "It certainly looks good," she told Abigail. "I hope you had an enjoyable afternoon."

Abigail smiled. "I did. As much as I need the shooting practice, I also needed a break."

Mrs. Baker stepped forward and put her arms around Abigail. "You poor dear. I can only imagine what you are going through. But don't you worry—Mr. Diamond is looking out for you, as well as the other men in this town." She patted the Derringer in her skirt pocket. "Not to mention I won't hesitate to shoot the fool," she added.

It took all Abigail's effort not to smile. She couldn't picture this dear lady shooting an attacker. "Have you ever shot anyone?" Abigail had to ask. Both their lives could depend on it.

"Well, no, I haven't, but I will if it's needed."

Abigail knew Mrs. Baker believed her own words. Despite all the training she'd had over the past days, Abigail still wasn't certain she could shoot someone. Her heart pounded in her ears. She knew she could pull the trigger on tin cans, but what about on an attacking man?

She closed her eyes momentarily, trying to picture herself on the defensive. Where she would be now if she hadn't escaped, Abigail didn't know. If these sweet people hadn't taken her in, she could be in dire straits. She needed distracting from her own miserable thoughts.

Mrs. Baker pulled down three mugs and made hot beverages for them all. "Mr. Diamond," she called. "Sit yourself down. I have freshly baked goodies." She raised her eyebrows at Abigail and smiled. Then she made coffee for Ben and tea for the two of them, then plated up some of the Christmas treats they'd made earlier.

Ben's eyes lit up as they entered the dining room. Anyone would think the man hadn't eaten for days. Abigail now understood what Mrs. Baker meant about men needing good food. It seemed food was the way to a man's heart.

Once they were all seated, Abigail glanced about. "With all the chaos, Christmas crept up on me," she said, her words sounding sad even to her own ears.

Mrs. Baker reached over and covered her hand. "We'll do our best to bring back your Christmas spirit," the older woman told her. Abigail knew she would be true to her word. "Eat up, everyone. They're better warm."

Ben didn't have to be told twice. Abigail watched his face as he tucked in. It was obvious he enjoyed Mrs. Baker's cooking. The woman was an excellent cook, that was plain to see. If Abigail could reach similar heights with her cooking skills, she would be extremely happy.

She glanced out the window. The snow was far heavier than before. "Does this mean…?"

Abigail didn't get to finish the sentence, as Mrs. Baker interrupted. "It's almost here. That pounding snow is the first indication of the blizzard coming. I need to check my stores and ensure we have enough food to get us through the next few days." She swung into action then, amazing Abigail at her agility. For a woman who must be several years north of seventy, she moved quickly and with ease. She went straight to her pantry and made a list of items she may need over the following days.

Next, she checked the icebox. "Milk and butter," she said out loud. "I must get to the mercantile," she said, speaking far quicker than Abigail had heard before.

"Is there such an urgency?" Abigail asked, wondering if it was a silly question.

Mrs. Baker didn't flinch and didn't treat her like the fool she felt herself to be. "Blizzards, my dear, are indiscriminate. They will hit at any moment, and will last as long as they wish. The moment it hits, we'll be stuck inside until it's over."

Abigail felt a shiver go down her spine. Mrs. Baker made it sound as though it could be a life and death situation. As though one such scenario wasn't enough for her to deal with.

"My Henry, may God rest his soul, built this cottage with his own hands. It will withstand any blizzard. It already did so once, and I'm certain it will do it again." She put her hands to her heart then, and Abigail was certain the older woman was thinking of better times when her husband was alive. She suddenly turned and hurried toward the front door, snatching up her coat and gloves. Abigail watched as she rushed toward the mercantile with her list held tightly in her hands.

She turned to Ben, who had said nothing during all this planning. He shrugged his shoulders. "I'm sure she knows what she's doing," he told Abigail. "It might have been a long time ago, but Mrs. Baker has endured one blizzard and came through it unscathed."

Abigail hoped it kept Samuel Bosworth at bay for another few days. Perhaps long enough for everyone to enjoy Christmas once the blizzard passed. Until then, she would be on high alert, as she was certain Ben, her protector and now dear friend, had been since the moment he'd heard her story.

Whether they all got through it was the question. She hoped and prayed Samuel could not find her.

On the other hand, she had no intention of looking over her shoulder for the rest of her life.

Chapter Thirteen

Ben stood behind Abigail and watched Mrs. Baker hurry through the snow toward the mercantile. She was nothing if not independent. Not that it wasn't an excellent trait. Of course it was, but he worried for the dear lady. She'd looked out for him for as long as Ben could remember. When he'd lost his mother, she had ensured his well-being. When he'd decided to set up his stagecoach business, she had urged him to push forward, despite the difficulties she knew he would face.

Now he had a thriving business, despite the obstacles he'd faced along the way. Such as the one he had recently endured. Whether his stagecoach would be in one piece after the blizzard threatening them would remain to be seen.

"I hope she will be alright," Abigail said, bringing him out of his thoughts. Then she turned to face him. They had never been this close before. Even when he'd been instructing her on how to shoot a gun, Ben had ensured he kept his distance. Propriety demanded it.

Only now, being only a whisper away meant he could make the slightest of movements and his lips would be over Abigail's. He glanced down at her face. Her gray eyes opened wide in astonishment, but she made no effort to move out of his reach.

Ben's heart fluttered at the prospect of kissing her, but he knew it was not the right thing to do. To be honest, they shouldn't be here, in this cottage, alone. Circumstances demanded otherwise. Mrs. Baker knew Abigail could not be left unprotected. The older woman knew how to shoot, but two women against a deranged man was asking for trouble.

From what Abigail had told him, the man was every bit as tall as Ben was, and muscular as well. He was no doubt capable of disabling both of them in a heartbeat. The thought had Ben's heart pounding. He must do everything in his power to protect Abigail.

As he stared down into her face, he saw her sadness. Her eyes pooled with unshed tears, and her mouth drooped. He much preferred to see her smile than to see her so unhappy. Not that he blamed her. It was not as though her life was going well right at this moment.

While his mind was telling him to step away and keep his distance, his heart forced him to put his arms around her and pull Abigail close. As she leaned against his chest, her warmth comforted him. Not that he was the one in danger. He'd known from the moment she'd handed him her ticket back in Devil's Edge there was something special about her. He'd also sensed there was something not quite right with the beautiful young woman he'd helped up the steps of the stage.

It had bothered him the entire time they'd traveled. Now he knew her story, all the terrible details of it, and he wanted to protect her from a man who was living in a fantasy world. A man who believed he could conjure up a scenario in his mind, and it would come to life. And that would have been fine, provided he hadn't included an innocent woman in his plans.

Of their own volition, Ben's arms came further up Abigail's back. Her warmth was better than anything he had encountered before. He could stand here like this all day, but knew the moment Mrs. Baker returned, he would feel her wrath. Or perhaps it would be the complete opposite.

You never could tell with Mrs. Baker. She was the self-appointed matchmaker of Grand Falls. Always had been for as long as Ben could remember.

He felt Abigail move against him. Glancing down, he stared into her beautiful face. It was covered in pain, and in sadness, but she would always be beautiful to him. Suddenly her tongue flicked out, and she licked her lips. It was Ben's undoing.

He leaned in and kissed her gently. His hands went up and cupped her face, and he deepened the kiss. It was at that moment the front door flew open.

"What is going on here?" Mrs. Baker demanded. But when he glanced up, he couldn't help but see the grin on her face.

"I…" Ben wasn't sure what to say. Nor did he think the question was said in all seriousness. He truly believed Mrs. Baker was ecstatic about this turn of events.

The older woman waved a hand across in front of herself. Then she laughed. "Someone will deliver my order shortly. I'll need help to store everything. After that…well, I'm certain I can find a way to fill our bellies." And just like that, she hurried into her cozy kitchen.

Whether Mrs. Baker felt the need to leave them alone, Ben wasn't sure. The sad fact of the matter was there would be a certain awkwardness between himself and Abigail now. At least he thought so. Whether Abigail did was another thing entirely.

Abigail glanced up at him, a small smile on her face. "That was nice," she whispered, then hurried to catch up with Mrs. Baker.

He couldn't help the grin that surely covered his entire face.

As darkness fell, an eerie quiet seemed to befall them. Ben pulled the window coverings aside and glanced outside. Snow swirled around, and the wind was far stronger than earlier. A storm was brewing, he had no doubt. Was the blizzard preparing to hit Grand Falls?

He had already secured the barn, and his horses were safe at the livery. His job now was to keep these ladies safe from the blizzard. Surely even someone as deranged as Samuel Bosworth wouldn't travel in this weather?

He heard the front door unlock. "Mrs. Baker," he called urgently. "Where are you going?" He hurried across the room to detain her. The petite woman would not have a chance in the strong winds.

"I forgot to close the shutters," she told him as she opened the door. Snow suddenly covered the floor.

"I'll go," he told her, ushering the elderly woman back inside. She frowned at him, and Ben felt her wrath without Mrs. Baker uttering a word.

"Thank you, dear," she said, her face softening. "The blizzard surely could have waited until after Christmas?"

Ben chuckled. Blizzards waited for no one, and they both knew it. He snatched up his thick coat and heavy gloves, and went outside. The wind was thunderous. And fierce. It took all his effort to take the few steps to the first window. How Mrs. Baker thought she would manage, he didn't know. She would have been blown away like a feather.

Having secured the first shutters, he moved to the next window and made his way around the cottage. He was more than a little relieved to get back inside. "All done," he announced upon his arrival inside. Ben removed his coat and gloves, then moved to the roaring fire. It wasn't long before a hot mug of coffee landed in his hands. "Thank you, Mrs. Baker," he said. "This will warm me up."

"It is I who should thank you. I didn't realize how bad it was outside." Ben could see the terror written on the woman's face. Perhaps she now understood the consequences she may have faced doing that task herself. "There's a stew on the stove, and it won't be much longer. Until then, rest up. I have a feeling tonight will not be easy for any of us."

She was right. If the weather of the moment was any sign, the blizzard was about to hit. He'd secured all the shutters, and packed away all the loose items in Mrs. Baker's small backyard. He would hate to see her freestanding wooden bench damage another person's home, or even injure someone.

Because he was away so much, there was little around his own home that would cause injury. The situation right now meant he wasn't leaving here to find out, no matter the consequences. Ben took a sip of the coffee. As always, Mrs. Baker's coffee was the best there was.

"The bread is ready," Abigail called from the kitchen. Mrs. Baker frowned. Ben had quickly learned she didn't like shouting, despite the occasional slip of the tongue herself. She hurried into the kitchen.

He followed her there, for no other reason than to enjoy the aroma of freshly cooked bread. Standing in the doorway with his mug of coffee, Ben breathed deeply. The smells were delightful. He wondered if he would ever have a wife with the cooking skills of Mrs. Baker.

Ben shook himself mentally. In all the years he'd been running his stagecoach business, he'd purposely kept his distance from women. It wasn't like he spent a lot of time at home, because he didn't. On the road, traveling sometimes for months at a time was not conducive to a happy marriage.

Not that he'd met the right person before, but now, praise the Lord, that had changed. Abigail Brooks had changed his way of thinking about marriage. And yet, his working situation had not changed.

He shook himself mentally. The fact he'd kissed her briefly did not mean he was promising a marriage. It also didn't mean Abigail was even interested in a relationship with him. Or any man. Especially after what she'd been through recently.

His timing was all wrong. The best thing he could do for both of them was to keep his distance. He was certain Abigail would appreciate it, too.

Chapter

Fourteen

Abigail awoke from a fitful sleep.

The rattle of shutters and the furious winds were not conducive to a good night's sleep. She had no idea what time it was—the closed shutters saw to that. She carefully found the lantern on the side table and lit it. The last thing she wanted to do was cause a fire.

With the room lit up, she could now see what she was doing, and quickly dressed with a view to making a cup of tea. Hopefully, she could move quietly enough not to wake Ben. If he managed to sleep, that was.

She carefully opened her bedroom door and crept to the kitchen, lantern still in her hands. Abigail knew the blizzard had hit, but as to its ferocity, she wasn't certain. The constant rattling of the shutters was unnerving, to say the least.

As she moved down the tiny hallway toward the sitting room, she noticed the silhouette of Ben crouched down at the fire. He seemed to add logs to it and glanced up as she came toward him. Poker in hand, he stoked the fire, causing the flames to flare.

He glanced her way momentarily. "I guess you couldn't sleep either," he said, then replaced the poker beside the fireplace, then stood.

"Not really," Abigail whispered, trying not to disturb Mrs. Baker. "I was about to make tea. Would you like coffee?"

"I'd prefer tea this time of night. Might as well sleep if I can." He scrubbed a hand across his chin then, and the action sent a thrill down her spine. What it was about this man, Abigail didn't know. What she knew was despite all that had happened with Samuel, she would happily spend the rest of her days with Benjamin Diamond.

It was clear he was a man of great morals. He was kind, and he had taken it upon himself to protect her. The mere fact he'd kissed her told Abigail she meant as much to him as he did to her.

She stepped toward him and placed the lantern on a side table. "I'll make the tea," she said, but he blocked her way.

"About before," he whispered, his breath warm on her face.

Abigail stared up at him and noticed his eyes shining in the fire's light. Was he having second thoughts? She couldn't blame him if he was. Samuel put her in a dangerous position, and she didn't want people she loved in a precarious situation because of her.

She gasped. Was she in love with Ben? Her heart fluttered at the mere thought of his earlier kiss. Except he didn't love her back. She'd heard about the passion of men. Many could not control their thoughts or their actions. Like Samuel.

Except Abigail knew Ben wasn't like that. He seemed far removed from her kidnapper and his behavior. "I'm sorry," she whispered into the semi-darkness. "I shouldn't have allowed things to get out of hand."

The words were barely out of her mouth when a muffled boom hit close by. She startled and moved to Ben for comfort. His arms quickly went around her. "I believe we're in the thick of it now," he said, his warmth and his arms giving her the comfort she craved.

Only Abigail knew this was not about comfort from the elements outside. There was far more to it. She might try to suppress her feelings, but it was near impossible. Her head rested on his chest, and his arms went tighter.

The sounds of wind and snow pounding on the front door as well as the shutters frightened her. Abigail had been in snowstorms, of course she had. But this was a whole new level of terrifying. Wind whistled through the shutters, and the lantern suddenly went out. "It will be alright," Ben whispered through the darkness.

With him holding her like this, Abigail knew his words to be true.

Suddenly, Mrs. Baker appeared out of nowhere. She was in her robe and seemed startled. "The blizzard has arrived," she said firmly, glancing from one to the other of them.

"I was about to make tea," Abigail said, no longer whispering.

Mrs. Baker grinned. "I can see that," she said, then hurried into the kitchen. Abigail glanced up at Ben, who was smiling. Why did everyone think it was funny? She certainly didn't. Losing her heart to a man she barely knew was not a good idea. Samuel had courted her for months, and look how that turned out.

Abigail sighed, then followed Mrs. Baker into her warm kitchen. Her woodstove was always loaded and burning. Abigail now understood why—the woman would bake at a whim, so needed her oven ready when she wanted it. With her lantern turned high, Mrs. Baker already had ingredients surrounding her. Perhaps it calmed her? Abigail would probably never know.

"Hot biscuits fix everything," she said, turning to face Abigail, then went back to her baking. Abigail wished she had the resolve of the widow who had opened her home to a stranger. She'd not even flinched when she learned of the danger it placed her in. Instead, she'd grabbed it with both hands, and stared it in the face. "Would you mind sprinkling the tray with flour?" she asked, and Abigail did as requested. Not once had she seen any biscuits stick during the cooking process while she'd been here.

Mrs. Baker had many cooking tricks she'd been sharing with Abigail since she'd arrived. She certainly appreciated it. If she ever became half the cook Mrs. Baker was, Abigail would be extremely happy.

How the woman stayed so carefree with a blizzard surrounding them, Abigail did not know. It was, however, rubbing off on her. When she'd awoken, Abigail was frightened and stressed. Between Ben holding her close, and Mrs. Baker making her biscuits, a certain calm had overtaken her.

At least Mrs. Baker's wish had come to fruition—she had prayed the blizzard would avoid Christmas day, and provided it didn't linger, her wish had been granted. Suddenly, there was a massive boom. The two women jumped, then embraced.

Ben entered the kitchen, glancing about, watching them hugging each other. They separated without so much as a word.

He walked down a hallway to the back of the cottage, returning less than a minute later. "One shutter out back has been torn off," he told them. Instead of reassuring her, it worried Abigail more.

"Don't even think about going outside to fix it," Mrs. Baker demanded. "It is not worth your life."

She watched as Ben studied the older woman momentarily. "I wouldn't dream of it. With no shutter there, you can see the extent of the storm. It's not good," he said, then walked toward the sink with his mug. Abigail took it from him. Their hands brushed, and a thrill ran down her spine. Her heart fluttered. Their eyes met, and Abigail knew what she felt was more than friendship. It was also more than gratefulness for Ben protecting her.

There was far more to this than she'd originally thought.

Chapter Fifteen

Ben shivered.

How could the mere act of passing over a mug cause him to feel this way? It made him wonder if Abigail had felt it, too. Ben shook himself mentally. Surely not.

Besides, the blizzard had him on high alert. Had it affected his senses, too?

As much as he tried to appear calm for the sake of the women, he was worried. He knew this cottage had been through a blizzard before, but could it withstand a second hammering from such a violent storm as this?

There was little he could do about it, but he had no intention of airing his concerns and scaring the women.

The sound of the oven door closing brought him back to the present. Mrs. Baker's hot biscuits would be most welcomed. He hadn't eaten so well as since he'd moved into the small cottage. Ben knew what a terrific cook Mrs. Baker was, as he'd eaten at the diner several times over the years. He was certain he would have eaten there far more if he didn't lead such a transient life.

His eyes sought Abigail. She was watching every move their hostess made, and now helped with the cleanup. As often as he offered to help, his help was always rejected. It was nice to simply sit back and take it easy, but Ben didn't have that luxury, despite it appearing that way.

When he wasn't listening to what the storm was doing, he was watching for Abigail's kidnapper. He had a vague idea what the man looked like, but being given a description wasn't the same as having a photograph or knowing them personally. He would hate to shoot the wrong attacker.

The thought almost made him smile. Surely there was only one person pursuing Abigail? He glanced at her again. This time, their eyes met, and his heart melted. How could someone who was effectively a stranger cause him to lose his heart so quickly? It wasn't like he'd shared a carriage with her. He might as well have been a hundred miles away. They were so far removed from each other.

He sighed. Abigail frowned. And Mrs. Baker turned to face him. "Is everything alright, Mr. Diamond?" she asked in her usual blunt fashion.

In the future, he would need to be far more careful. "Perfectly, thank you. I'm tired, that's all."

The older woman rolled her eyes. "Aren't we all?" She smiled then and went back to her soapy water.

Ben leaned back against the kitchen wall. He wasn't sure what it was—the aromas, the warmth, or perhaps the fact Abigail Brooks was there—but he always felt at home in that tiny kitchen. It was funny, really; he pictured Mrs. Baker having a far bigger kitchen. Something like the diner. He realized now it was a silly assumption, since she lived alone. When the cottage was built, her husband lived there too, but it was a perfectly sized kitchen for a cottage of this size. His cottage was larger. It had been built with his future in mind. One that included a wife and several children.

His gaze went to Abigail again.

Ben shook his head, then stormed out of the room. He was obviously bored. His thoughts would not be going down that track otherwise. He made himself comfortable in one of the luxurious chairs Mrs. Baker had in her sitting room. Her home was the height of luxury. And why not? She'd worked hard all her life until she'd handed her precious diner over to Tucker and Maggie Smith. Of course, they weren't married then, but they are now.

Ben suddenly stood. He was apparently far more sleep deprived than he realized. He glanced about the room. The fire. It needed stoking. Didn't it? Anything to try to keep him awake. Ben loaded more logs onto the fire, then stoked it to get the flames moving. He was pleased he'd brought plenty of wood inside before the storm. It should last until it was all over.

That task over and done with, he sat himself back on the same chair he'd sat in a short time ago. He closed his eyes briefly while he waited for the ladies to join him.

Ben awoke to quiet giggling. Rarely, he'd heard Abigail laugh. He truly enjoyed the sound. He blinked, then glanced about.

"Ah, Mr. Diamond. You're awake." Mrs. Baker's voice held a hint of laughter. "It's a wonder your snoring didn't wake you earlier."

Snoring? He didn't snore. Did he? "I apologize, ladies," he said, trying not to sound gruff. He wondered how long he'd slept and glanced at his pocket watch. Around a quarter of an hour. Not long in the scheme of things, but long enough to take the edge off his fatigue.

"Join us, Mr. Diamond, while the biscuits are still hot." Mrs. Baker patted the dining room chair next to her, showing where he should sit. That it happened to be next to Abigail as well was no coincidence, he was certain.

"Your biscuits smell delicious," he said as he took his place at the table.

"They are," Abigail told him, then pushed a plate loaded with butter toward him. She smiled and his heart fluttered. Surely the fact he was still half asleep caused it to happen? Only Ben knew the truth. It was not sleep deprivation causing his reactions. He had fallen head and heart in love with Abigail Brooks.

"Are you still with us, Mr. Diamond?" Mrs. Baker's words alerted him to the fact he was staring at Abigail. Her big smile and her kind heart had drawn him to her. The time they'd spent together, not only while he taught her to shoot, but here in this cozy cottage—that's really what was to blame.

Their proximity meant he'd gotten to know Abigail far better than he'd ever intended. From the moment he learned of her situation, Ben knew he had to help. Since then, he'd spent practically every waking moment doing exactly that.

As he buttered a hot biscuit, his mind ticked over at a million miles an hour. He still hadn't come up with a plan, should Samuel Bosworth have the audacity to show up in Grand Falls. From what he'd heard, nothing would be beyond him.

The moment the freshly baked biscuit hit his taste buds, Ben was in heaven. He stared at Mrs. Baker, his mouth still full, and nodded. "Your cooking never ceases to amaze me, Mrs. Baker," he said once his mouth was empty.

"Have another," she told him, and pushed the plate closer to him. "There's nothing more satisfying than to see a man enjoying the food you've created." She winked at Abigail, who tried to hide her smile, but failed miserably.

"I hope to one day be able to cook that well." Abigail glanced at her hands, giving Ben the impression she didn't believe it was something she could ever achieve.

"My dear girl," Mrs. Baker said. "We'll make a decent cook of you yet." She glanced toward Ben then. "If only for your future husband's sake."

Ben's heart thudded at the words that shocked him, but knew deep down, he'd be more than happy to have Abigail as his wife.

Chapter Sixteen

Lightning flashed outside, causing the room to light up now and then. There was a massive clap of thunder, whereas earlier, the storm had muffled it.

Now quiet surrounded them. It was surreal. Not a sound could be heard—not even a bird chirped. Abigail was suddenly afraid. She did not know why—there appeared to be nothing to frighten her. After all, it seemed to be the lull that often occurred after a massive storm.

The sound of a shutter flapping caught Abigail's attention. It came from the dining room. At least that's where it sounded to be coming from. She walked over to the window and glanced outside at the small area that was visible.

Everything was white. The ground was completely covered; the stores were all covered too. There was not a gap anywhere in sight. The little she could see appeared magical. It also hurt her eyes. Far too much snow and the sun peeked through the few clouds left in the sky. That, bounced off the mounds of snow scattered about.

"It's beautiful," she said, more to herself than anyone else. Then Abigail ran to the front door. She wanted to take in the full beauty of it all.

"Abigail, don't!" Ben called to her as she unlocked the door. "You don't know what, or who, is out there."

But it was too late. She'd already opened the door. Snow fell inside and covered her boots. She kicked it off, then glanced up, planning to take in all the beauty of Grand Falls after a blizzard.

Her heart thudded. His back was toward her, but there was no doubt in Abigail's mind. Samuel Bosworth stood in the middle of Grand Falls. Looking for her, no doubt. She tried to slam the door shut, but the snow made it impossible. She gasped, then slid her hand into her skirt pocket, reassuring herself the Derringer was still there. It was fully loaded, but two bullets may not keep her alive. Or Ben. Or Mrs. Baker.

Ben hurried to her side. "Is it him?" he whispered.

She couldn't speak, but nodded her head. It was then she knew what Ben had tried to tell her—when the time came, she might find herself frozen in fear. Indeed, that's what was happening. Despite her heart thudding, and her entire body trembling with fear, Abigail was determined this monster would not get away with what he did to her.

"What do you want?" she shouted to him, and Samuel spun around in the snow as best he could. As he turned, he fell forward. If the situation hadn't been so serious, it would have been comical.

"Don't antagonize him," Ben whispered, pushing her behind himself.

Only moments later, Abigail's kidnapper lifted the Colt he had in his hand. How she had not noticed it, she did not know. "I want you, my darling," he said sweetly. If she hadn't learned the hard way of his true personality, Abigail would believe he was a kind and caring man. Heck, he tricked her into believing it once before.

"Put the gun down, and back away," Ben said firmly.

But it only seemed to anger Samuel. "Who are you?" he demanded. "I'm her fiancé."

Abigail was astounded. Did he really tell Ben an absolute lie? "The moment you kidnapped me, our engagement was broken," she shouted, then wished she hadn't spoken at all.

Samuel's face contorted, and his hand shook with rage. He took a step toward the cottage. Then another. All the time, his hand shook. Even if he fired the gun, who knew what or who he would hit?

"Get back inside," Ben demanded.

Fury filled Abigail. Did he think she'd spent all that time learning to shoot only to back away when threatened by this... bully? Samuel took another step forward. The deep snow made it slow going, which was definitely a blessing. It meant he couldn't get close quickly.

It was then Abigail noticed Mrs. Baker was missing from the room. Where was she? "Mrs. Baker is gone," Abigail whispered to Ben.

"Probably gone further back into the cottage, which is exactly what you need to do. It's safer there." She could hear the anger in his voice, although he whispered. Whether it was aimed at her or Samuel, she would probably never know.

Suddenly, and without warning, Abigail's ears rang. Samuel had fired his gun and stood there grinning, not fifteen feet away. Ben reeled back, and blood flowed from his shoulder. She reached into her skirt pocket, pulled out the Derringer, and without hesitation, pulled the trigger. Not once, but twice.

Samuel still stood. Suddenly, another shot rang out, and another. Abigail didn't know where it came from, but knew she had to do something or he would kill them all. Ben was endeavoring to get to his feet, but stumbled. She snatched up the Colt from his hands and fired. The first shot hit Samuel's shoulder. He stumbled backwards but righted himself.

Abigail took a steadying breath, knowing this time she had to knock him to the ground. Permanently. The thought of killing another human being pained her. She silently prayed to God for his guidance. She also asked for his forgiveness for what she was about to do.

Abigail glanced at the snow that had turned red. Her heart pounded and her hands were sweaty. She held the Colt in both hands and aimed. Samuel laughed.

Until she pulled the trigger.

 ~*~

Sheriff Earl Saxon was first on the scene. He quickly removed her attacker's gun, then checked the man's pulse.

Trudging through the snow, he made his way toward Abigail. He glanced across to Ben, who was being looked after by Mrs. Baker. Abigail stood frozen to the spot. Had she really pulled the trigger and erased a man's life?

"Abigail," Ben's voice barely penetrated the fog currently filling her mind. Someone, she wasn't certain if it was the sheriff or Ben Diamond, or someone else entirely, took the Colt from her hands. The next moment, she was cradled in Ben's arms.

"For goodness' sake, Mr. Diamond. At least let me bandage your injury." Mrs. Baker's voice was filled with frustration.

Ben ignored her. "Abigail? The sheriff is here," he said gently, then wiped a thumb across her face. Not that Abigail knew she was crying. Where had those tears come from?

He led her across to one of the comfortable chairs in Mrs. Baker's cozy cottage. The fire was roaring, but the door was wide open. It seemed like a contradiction to Abigail and she laughed. Tears continued to flood her cheeks as she did so.

Mrs. Baker shoved a mug of hot tea toward her. Abigail stared down into it but didn't take it and didn't drink any. It was like she was in a daze.

"She's in shock," Sheriff Saxon said. "I'll get Doc Spencer to check her over. He needs to look at that shoulder of yours as well." Did that mean he was talking to Ben? Abigail glanced about the room. It seemed to be full of people. The noise was deafening, but not as loud as the gunshot.

Suddenly, she remembered something. "Where did those other two shots come from?" she asked, confusion hitting her.

Ben and the sheriff glanced at each other. "No idea," Sheriff Saxon told her, then glanced about, no doubt looking for another shooter.

When Abigail glanced at Mrs. Baker, she noticed the woman was ghostly white. Surely it couldn't be?

"I shot him. Little good it did." The dear lady appeared distraught, but without her help, would they all still be here now? "I'm not sorry, either. I'm only sorry I didn't kill him. It would have saved this dear girl the grief."

Abigail knew Mrs. Baker was feisty, but had no idea exactly how far she would go to save her friends.

Chapter

Seventeen

Ben stared at Mrs. Baker. Perhaps she was in shock as well? Surely this elderly woman did not, moments ago, try to kill Abigail's attacker?

Even as the thought entered his head, he knew it was true. According to the sheriff, there was no one else to be found. Mrs. Baker had disappeared to who knew where. And…they now knew she carried a Derringer in her pocket.

Good on her for giving it her best shot. Ben chuckled at his pun, despite the situation being less than stellar.

Without warning, Mrs. Baker snatched up a broom and tried to coerce the melting snow that sat just inside her front door into going back where it belonged. It didn't work. He could see her frustration, but he was a little busy trying to stem the flow of blood from his shoulder right at this moment.

Suddenly, Abigail jumped up from her chair. She pushed him into the beautifully embroidered chair Ben thought might be a family heirloom. He resisted. "I don't want to get blood on Mrs. Baker's beautiful chair," he said, standing his ground. Standing his ground, Abigail could not physically move him.

Mrs. Baker stared at him. "Do as you're told, Mr. Diamond. I'd rather that than have to pick you up off the floor. That might be rather difficult." She smirked then, and he knew the elderly woman would be alright.

Suddenly, Doc Spencer hurried into the cottage. "Your man outside is gone," he said, then headed toward Ben.

"I'd rather you checked the ladies first," he told the doctor, but his advice went unheeded.

Doctor Spencer opened his medical bag and rummaged through it. "Hold that towel on there, would you?" he asked to anyone who would listen. Abigail moved forward and gripped the blood-soaked towel. After examining Ben's shoulder, the doc cleaned it, then bandaged it. "The bullet went straight through. You're a lucky man." Ben knew he was. It could have been a far worse outcome.

"You might find a bullet in your wall, Mrs. Baker. Depending on where Mr. Diamond was standing," the doctor said, then moved toward Abigail despite her protests. "It's shock. Rest and a good hot cup of tea will help," he said, then moved onto Mrs. Baker. The diagnosis was the same.

Soon, the room was cleared. Sheriff Saxon followed the doctor out, and arranged for Samuel Bosworth's body to be removed immediately. Abigail hurried into the kitchen while Mrs. Baker closed the front door after giving up on cleaning up the mess from the melting snow.

When they all sat around the table, mugs in hand, pound cake in front of them, Ben pondered the day, the dire consequences, and what might have been.

No one spoke. He figured they were all still rather shocked at the confrontation that had occurred today. He always knew there was a possibility the deranged man would eventually turn up, but wondered how he'd got through while a storm was raging. The only feasible answer he could come up with was he'd arrived before the blizzard.

The very thought of it made Ben shiver.

"Are you cold, Mr. Diamond?" Mrs. Baker asked quietly. "I'll stoke the fire." She stood, but he waved her down.

"I can do it," he said. Ben had no intention of airing his suspicions with the two shocked women. They already had enough to contend with from today's events. They certainly didn't need to know the deranged killer may have been hiding out in plain sight.

A few days later, and Christmas day arrived. Tucker invited all his friends to the diner for Christmas lunch. That included Mrs. Baker, Abigail, and Ben.

They had pushed together several tables, so everyone was on the same table. It was a wonderful gesture, and certainly one he appreciated. He believed the others did, too.

It was cozy, and the atmosphere was electric. Ben knew all the guests, and most everyone knew each other. Abigail seemed pleased to see the sisters and the preacher who had begun this journey with her.

With the recent drama they'd endured, not to mention the blizzard, the stagecoach still lay where it was damaged. Whether it would be salvageable would be another question entirely. Of course, he could always start from scratch with another coach. If he decided that was the path he wanted to pursue. Right now, he had other things on his mind.

"A word, if you don't mind," Mrs. Baker said once everyone was seated, then stood. She glanced from one person to another. "I've lived in this charming town all my life. It's always been a caring community, and a place where everyone looked after one another." Ben wondered if she was going to berate how much it had changed over the years, although he couldn't agree. "I am very pleased to say nothing has changed," she said, surprising him. "Thank you all for rallying around Miss Brooks when she needed you most." Mrs. Baker had tears in her eyes and sat down before she allowed them to fall.

Ben stood next. "It's my turn to speak," he said, his heart pounding, and his legs like jelly beneath him. "I've come to know Abigail Brooks well. I can happily share she is a woman with conviction. To be honest, I don't know where she gets her strength from." Ben shook his head. "But I digress. Abigail," he said, turning to face her. "Thank you for saving my life. Mrs. Baker, I didn't know you had it in you. My thanks go to you as well."

A few chuckles went around the table at his last statement.

Ben stepped away from the table and the place where he'd been seated. He reached out to Abigail and brought her to standing. "This might not be the right time after all that's happened, but I'm going to say it, anyway." He took a long fortifying breath, then studied her. "Abigail, I know we haven't known each other very long. However, I've come to care deeply for you, and truly love you." Abigail gasped, and he was certain she'd guessed his intent. Still, he continued. "To the point, I can't imagine my life without you. Abigail Brooks, will you marry me?"

Now the words were out, he waited for Abigail to answer.

Abigail stared down at him, and it felt like a lifetime. Of course it was only moments. Ben's heart pounded, and he was certain he would keel over and make a fool of himself before too long.

What if she said no?

It wasn't a possibility he'd even considered. But what if she did? Not only would it break his heart, he would look like the biggest idiot Grand Falls ever saw.

She squeezed his hand, and Ben glanced up. His heart pounded so loudly he was certain even if she spoke he wouldn't hear her.

Abigail studied him. Was she contemplating her answer, how to reject his proposal? Or would she simply walk out the door, never to be seen again?

Now Ben knew he was overreacting. There was no stagecoach because it was laying somewhere outside Grand Falls waiting for further assessment.

There was always the train, but that still couldn't go anywhere.

He wanted to run. Where to? He did not know, but now he wanted to take it all back. Pretend he hadn't asked the one thing of a woman he'd never asked before.

His heart was aching. Why didn't she answer him?

Ben glanced around the room. Everyone was watching, waiting. He felt like an insect under glass. Everything was moving in slow motion and he wanted time to move quicker. Only for now, though, to get it over and done with.

"Ben," Abigail's sweet voice fractured his thoughts. "I love you too. Of course I will marry you."

Tears rolled down her cheeks, and Ben stood. He wiped her tears away, then pulled her close. He loved Abigail Brooks with all his heart and wanted to spend forever with her.

Ben heard the applause in the background and decided to ignore it. He lifted Abigail's chin and leaned down to kiss her thoroughly.

 *Epilogue*

Almost three years later…

Abigail sat in the corner of the sitting room, sipping tea, Mrs. Baker not far away. A brightly decorated Christmas tree was nearby.

Two-year-old James played quietly at Ben's feet, glancing at the tree now and then. Suddenly, he jumped up and headed for Mrs. Baker. "Read a story, grandma-ma?" he asked, and the older woman beamed.

Mrs. Baker was grandma-ma to many of the children in Grand Falls, and she treated them all equally. "Of course, dear boy," she told him, and reached for *Black Beauty*, a children's book James seemed to favor.

Ben sat back and watched in awe at his small but expanding family. Abigail rubbed a hand across her swollen belly, her expression one of pure happiness.

Despite the drama and difficulties they endured in the beginning, life had been good to them.

He'd given up driving the stagecoach and instead concentrated on the business side of things. It allowed him to spend far more time with his family, and in the town he loved so much.

He heard the book snap close, and his head shot up. Ben knew what came next—it was his turn to read to his precious son. This time, James brought his chosen book with him and climbed up on his father's knee.

"I'll check on the stew," Mrs. Baker told him, then headed to the kitchen. She was as independent as ever and still carried her Derringer in her skirt pocket. Abigail had retired her firearm, preferring not to have one where James might find it.

"Pinocchio," Ben began, and the boy giggled. This was a newly released book, and Ben had ordered it in especially for James' recent birthday.

"Pinocchio," James repeated, then settled in to listen.

Ben heard Abigail sigh. It seemed a sigh of contentment, and he knew very well how she was feeling. Almost three years ago, they faced the worst time of their lives, Abigail especially. But they'd made it through with the love of each other, and their prayers to God.

As he read the words from the much loved book, Ben silently thanked God for leading him to this moment, to Abigail, and to the love he never knew he possessed.

From the Author

Thank you so much for reading my book – I hope you enjoyed it.

I would greatly appreciate you leaving a review where you purchased, even if it is only a one-liner. It helps to have my books more visible!

About the Author

Multi-published, award-winning and bestselling author Cheryl Wright, former secretary, debt collector, account manager, writing coach, and shopping tour hostess, loves reading.

She writes both historical and contemporary western romance, as well as romantic suspense.

She lives in Melbourne, Australia, and is married with two adult children and has six grandchildren. When she's not writing, she can be found in her craft room making greeting cards.

Links

Website: *http://www.cheryl-wright.com/*

Facebook Reader Group:
https://www.facebook.com/groups/cherylwrightauthor/

Join My Newsletter:

https://cheryl-wright.com/newsletter/
(and receive a free book)